Let it Snow

COZY MYSTERIES FOR WINTER

DAISY LANDISH

Editing by Jessica McKenna
Cover by Daisy Landish

BEACHES AND TRAILS
PUBLISHING

ABOUT THE AUTHOR

Daisy Landish is a romance and cozy mystery author living in the UK, whose clean and sweet stories have tugged at readers' heartstrings across the pond and beyond. When she's not writing, Daisy spends her time reading, hiking at dawn, and riding into the sunset on her horse, Rosebud.

Join Daisy's Newsletter for updates and giveaways!
www.daisylandishromance.com

facebook.com/daisylandishromance

x.com/daisy_landish

instagram.com/beachesandtrailspublishing

amazon.com/author/daisylandish

bookbub.com/authors/daisy-landish

goodreads.com/Daisy_Landish

ALSO BY DAISY LANDISH

Clean Regency Romance

The Lady Series - The Allington Collection

The Lady Series - The Gillingham Collection

The Lady Series - The Blackmore Collection

The Lady Series - The Norrington Collection

Clean Contemporary Romance

Love on Spruce Island

Second Chance

Cherry Tree Island

The Wedding Trio

Extra Credit

Counting on the Cowboy

Focusing on the Cowboy

Mistletoe Magic

Grounded at Christmas

Cozy Mysteries

Jane and Kennedy Daniels Mysteries

Pine Grove Mysteries

Annie Archer Paranormal Mysteries

Wilma Wade Holiday Mysteries

Mike and Maddie Mysteries

Mystic Moonhaven Mysteries

Sweater Weather: Cozy Mysteries for Fall

Summer Vibes: Cozy Mysteries for Summer

Let it Snow: Cozy Mysteries for Winter

A LITTLE FROSTY

A MIKE AND MADDIE MYSTERY

PROLOGUE

Winter had officially set in over Coeur d'Alene, Idaho, with the slow build of snowfall. In the New Year, they had almost eight inches sitting on the ground. It was pretty incredible, mused the man as he stood at the top of a large hill.

This was one of the best places for children to go sledding during the day. The snow had been packed hard over the hill. Fortunately for the man, it had been snowing almost steadily over the last few days, giving a lovely fresh coating. He looked down at the body he had brought here and shook his head. It was a shame that everything had to end this way.

"Death," he said to the body, "is the only constant. Nothing else in the world can be as constant as it. People like to say 'death and taxes,' but if civilization were to fall, taxes would end. Death? No. It wouldn't. You could argue that life is a constant, but the dinosaurs would disagree."

He chuckled, although there really wasn't anything funny about the whole situation. A sort of nervousness ran through him as he pulled a spray bottle from his pocket and misted down the body.

At this time of night, nobody would come to this hill, not when it was so far out of town. But he still had to work quickly—no time for philosophical musings. Once the body was sufficiently damp, he started rolling it. The fresh snow clung to the body, the dampness melting the snow's top layers while simultaneously freezing.

With one last shove, the body rolled under its momentum, picking up more snow. By the time it reached a standstill at the bottom of the hill, it was nothing more than a fat cylinder of white.

Nodding in satisfaction, the man settled into a wide toboggan, aiming the nose of it so he would avoid the dead object. He chuckled as he moved his body back and forth, edging the toboggan into a full slide down the hill. The wind rushed in his ears, and he couldn't help but laugh loudly.

He slid past the body and put his hands out, digging into the snow to stop himself. He was still chuckling as he dragged the toboggan back and rolled the body onto it.

"I haven't gone sledding since I was a kid," he said to the body as he hauled it back up the hill. "Then again, I haven't made a snowman since I was a kid, either. But don't worry, Ned. I'll make something beautiful for you."

CHAPTER 1

Mike frowned at the door, propped slightly open, which led into his best friend's house. Maddie wasn't usually so careless about such things. He knocked on the doorframe and pushed the door open further.

"Miss Moreau, are you home?" he called into the apartment.

Maddie appeared around the corner that led to her kitchen, her brow furrowed. "Miss Moreau? What's that about?"

Mike was relieved to see her all right; all he did was shrug as he stepped inside. He unwound the scarf from around his neck and shut the door, relishing the warmth of Maddie's apartment. She always kept it warmer than what he thought was strictly necessary. But it was nice to wear shorts and a t-shirt all the same.

"Can't I call you Miss Moreau?" he teased. "It is your name."

Maddie faked a bow toward him. "By all means, Mr. Malison. Please, enter my humble abode."

Mike snorted. He hung up his coat and peeled off the sweater he'd worn to walk over. "Why did you have your door open?"

"Because I got a new lock. It locks automatically whenever the door gets shut, and I didn't want to be bothered to unlock it for you," Maddie shrugged as she headed back into the kitchen. "I figure we can get started on work over breakfast. This plot is giving me a hard time, and I want to get it done so I can do that art class."

"Is Carson joining us today?" Mike asked.

"No, he got called off to something else."

Perfect. Mike grinned as he shut the door. He usually enjoyed having the older man around. He was an excellent grounder when Mike and Maddie started too deep into their flights of fancy. Lately, however, the sheer number of cases that Detective Carson Luttrell brought to them impeded Mike and Maddie's day jobs.

Mike loved to solve mysteries. He loved to figure out the clues and put together a scenario of what happened. Unfortunately, Carson couldn't pay them for the work they did. He had tried to convince his police chief to hire the two as consultants but had been shot down immediately.

Maddie came from a wealthy family. She worked because she liked to stay busy and found great creative freedom in dreaming up the plots she wrote as a freelancer. Mike, on the other hand, relied on his ghostwriting income.

Oh, he wasn't hard up for money by a long shot. He had built himself quite a successful career and had enough savings so he could take on interesting projects. It was wise to keep an income coming in when he was able.

"Smells delicious," Mike said.

He went to the cupboards and began taking out the utensils as Maddie flipped French Toast on the stove. He inhaled deeply. While the scent of eggs and butter was both strong, there was something else he couldn't quite put his finger on.

Maddie covered the frying pan with a lid. "Don't look. I put in a secret ingredient. I want to see if you figure it out."

"Interesting," Mike grinned. They often did this, sneaking different ingredients into their food.

He set the table and prepared the coffee as Maddie finished cooking breakfast. She plated the food, put syrup and whipped cream on the toast, and brought it to the table. They sat down together, and Mike sniffed the meal again.

"Cinnamon?" he guessed.

"Yes, but that's not the secret."

"Hmmm." Mike studied his food. "I saw half a dozen snowmen in your front yard this morning. I don't recall seeing them yesterday."

"There's a snowman contest happening in the town. Several families were out there all day yesterday, fighting over who had the best claim to the snow." Maddie cut her toast elegantly as she shook her head, her chestnut-brown hair bouncing slightly. "I never understood what's so exciting about snowmen."

Mike chuckled. "That's because you never got snow where you grew up."

"Vancouver gets some snow," Maddie protested. "Just... not much. So the city isn't ever prepared for it, despite winter happening every year. So many times when there was nothing but a skiff of snow on the ground and everything shut down."

"Ah, but that's because you so rarely got snow. Why bother with winter tires if you don't have a winter?" Mike chewed his food thoughtfully, trying to figure out what he was tasting. "Nutmeg?"

Maddie grinned. "No."

He took another taste. Something was different; he knew that. But what? "In any case, I feel bad for you, Maddie. Building snowmen was the highlight of my childhood."

"The highlight, eh?"

Mike grinned. "Maybe it's because I grew up on a farm, and we had lots of space to build them. It was always a family affair. When the holidays rolled around, my cousins would always visit, and we would build the best snowmen you can imagine."

"Perfectly round, sparkling white, 'with a corncob pipe, a button nose, and two eyes made of coal?' Did you also have a magic top hat that brought him to life?" Maddie teased, quoting the words of 'Frosty the Snowman.'

"Frosty had nothing on our snowmen."

Maddie rolled her eyes, though she was still smiling. She sipped her coffee. "Do tell."

"One year, we all worked together on a single snowman. We used the tractor to lift the body and head because they were heavy." Mike smiled as he remembered those childhood days. "My dad carved a giant piece of wood and painted it to look like a carrot, and we tied all our old scarves together to get around its neck."

"Impressive."

Mike sat back, idly eating as the childhood memories swept through him. Perhaps his new pet project should collect snowman memories from his cousins and compile a book to gift them next Christmas.

"Another year," he continued, "we built a snowman around our playhouse. It kept everything cozy and warm inside, and we thought it was perfectly camouflaged from the outside."

Maddie propped her elbow on the table and rested her chin in her hand. "So, was the highlight really the snowmen or the memories you share with your cousins?"

"The snowmen are the symbols for the memories," Mike replied. "I'm sure I have some pictures of them somewhere. I'll bring them over tomorrow."

"That sounds delightful." Maddie's expression took on a wistful look.

"What's wrong?"

"I'm not sure," Maddie said slowly. "Ever since I went home to Vancouver over the holidays, I've been melancholy. Coeur d'Alene is such a beautiful little town. I love it here. But I miss Canada. I miss my family. I miss the ocean."

Mike took her hand in his and squeezed lightly. "Perhaps you're feeling unfulfilled in life?"

"Perhaps. My younger sister announced that she was pregnant. Twenty-six years old, married, with a child on the way. There was a time when I thought I would have that life. And here I am, thirty years old, without so much as a boyfriend," Maddie shook her head. "Not that I actually want that life. I thought I did when I was a teen, but thank goodness, I was exposed to other ideas. I don't like babies, as it turns out."

"No?" Mike's brow furrowed. Through the years he had known Maddie, he couldn't remember a time when they talked about dating, marriage, or children.

Maddie shook her head. "No. They stress me out too much. Oh, they're adorable, and I will be the best aunt I can. But if I ever decide to have children, I think I'll foster them or adopt."

"I see. But your younger sister achieving those goals you once wanted for yourself is making you doubt your place in life, now?" Mike pushed gently.

"I suppose it could be. Or perhaps it's just that I wish I could have the simple nostalgia of childhood," she shrugged. "Anyway, I'm sorry I interrupted your childhood memories to be so dreadfully woe-is-me." A smile blossomed across her face. "Do you have any other snowmen tales?"

Before Mike could reply, there was a knock on the door. They shared a startled glance before Maddie left to answer it. Moments later, she returned with Carson trailing after her. He had dark circles under his eyes and an overall haggard look.

"Sorry for interrupting," the detective said as he slumped into a car. "This missing person's case is taking a toll on me. We received another tip yesterday that has turned out to be nothing."

"Missing person?" Mike leaned forward. Though he knew he needed to work, his focus was instantly on this case's possibilities. "You mean Ned Vande, that TikToker who went missing last week?"

Carson nodded. Maddie was busy making a third cup of coffee, so Mike slid his plate of French toast to Carson. It looked like the detective needed it more than he did.

"I've seen stuff about that on the news. Is it true that you suspect his wife might be—" she turned around and cried out. "Don't eat that!"

Carson had just been about to put his first bite of French toast in his mouth. He dropped the fork, looking startled.

Maddie hurried over and took the plate away while giving Carson his coffee. "Sorry. But you're allergic."

"Oh!" Mike's eyes widened. He let out a laugh as he slapped his knee. "So that's the secret ingredient! You made it with soy eggs!"

CHAPTER 2

Maddie shook her head sadly as she got a new pan to cook Carson breakfast. He protested, telling her she didn't need to make any special effort for him, but she was feeling antsy today.

An extensive project was due; no matter how hard she pressed herself, her brain just didn't want to work. It was beyond frustrating. Maybe a break was just what she needed. This could be a symptom of winter, yes, but it could also be a creative burnout. Perhaps it would help if she took a page from Mike's book and took up a physical job for a while. It would give her a fresh experience, at the very least.

"Now," she said once she had finished Carson's favorite, bacon and avocado on rye toast, "is this missing person's case something you want help on, or are you looking for a distraction?"

Mike shot her a doe-eyed look. She rolled her eyes at him. That look meant he had already latched onto the idea of helping Carson with it and wasn't happy that she had suggested a different topic of conversation.

"I'm not sure," Carson hedged. He took a big bite of his toast and closed his eyes, humming in satisfaction.

"Ned Vande," Mike quickly said, taking advantage of Carson's silence. "He made himself famous on TikTok, right? He was that stay-at-home dad who built a brand around being a good father and partner. Right?"

Maddie returned to her food. She was disappointed that her 'surprise ingredient' had been blown the way it did, but the dish was still delicious. It was the first time she had served Mike a vegan meal—well, vegetarian; she supposed since she had used whipped cow's cream as a topping—that he hadn't guessed it straight off. She had planned to use it as a springboard to ask Mike his thoughts on her perhaps going into culinary school.

As much as she would love to have another mysterious case to help Detective Luttrell solve, she needed some life advice right now. She loved her life and work, but there was that little voice in the back of her mind saying she was stuck in a rut.

She pushed the voice away, concentrating on her two friends. "Wasn't there a huge controversy recently where it turned out he actually had a nanny taking care of the kids and was cheating on his wife?"

Carson nodded. "It's more than rumor. He used the income from his TikTok videos to hire the labor in the house and started an affair. With Vande being such a public figure, it quite opens up the possibilities. His wife claims he left with his affair partner, but there have been no charges on his credit cards, no sightings, and it's looking more and more like murder."

Right. Maddie reminded herself that it wasn't yet murder, only a missing person. She cut up a strawberry and dipped it in the cream before putting it in her mouth.

"The wife did it," Mike said.

"Too cliché," Maddie protested. She waved her fork at him. "The kids did it. They got sick of being put online and mistreated by their father and so ganged up together to do away with him."

Mike's eyes gleamed. "And the mom is covering for them?"

Maddie considered it. "No," she finally said. "She's not covering for them. She's a workaholic who's barely at home—"

"Cliché," Mike protested. "And makes it appear the mom being the breadwinner is why her husband cheated."

"True. But she's still not covering for them. She kicked her husband out of the house when she found out he was having an affair, and he went missing right after. She assumes he ran off with his affair partner. The truth of it, the kids did it, and the nanny knows."

Mike arched a brow at her. "The nanny? Why would she hide it?"

"Because she loves those kids and is terrified that if she steps forward, the police will think she did it. After all—"

"After all," Carson broke in, chuckling as he shook his head, "why bother with the facts when you can have a pleasant flight of fancy?"

Maddie stuck her tongue out at him. Sometimes she thought that Carson's interjections like this were exactly how a big brother would act with his younger siblings, making her want to act like his little sister.

"Fine, fine." Mike waved a hand. "Then tell us, Detective, what are the details of this case?"

"A week ago, news broke that Ned Vande was lying to all his followers. Instantly, his feeds were full of threats; most aren't serious and just people who are chronically online." Carson licked the bacon grease off his fingers, then wiped them on a napkin. "However, Vande disappeared that night."

Maddie nodded. "What does the wife say happened?"

"She states she left work early after seeing the news, to be there with her children. When she arrived, she found the children with a nanny and no sign of her husband. He was having an affair with a young woman named Jean Lune, but she claims not to have seen him for almost two weeks."

Mike gathered the empty plates. "And the nanny?"

"She says that when she arrived in the morning to look after the children, Vande left at once without telling her where he was going. He left his cell phone at home but took his wallet with him."

"So she is the last to see him alive," Maddie mentioned. She stood to clean up the dishes, but Mike waved his hand at her.

Mike set the dishes beside the sink. "I'm done my coffee, and you still have half a mug left. Let me wash these up while you relax, okay?"

Maddie sighed as she leaned back into her chair. "Very well. Back to Vande. The nanny was the last to see him alive. Has his car been found?"

"No. Unfortunately, that's about all we have. A traffic camera took a picture of him running a red light in Spokane later that night, but the image is so blurry we don't know if it was actually Vande driving. There's been no sign of the car after that, even though we have an APB out on it." Carson shook his head, looking tired again.

"Then he must have dumped it," Mike concluded.

"Or he's dead," Maddie pointed out. "Or perhaps he's hiding low in a friend's rural cabin, or he went to Canada."

"In any case," Carson said as he stood from the table. "I don't want you two wrapping yourselves up in this case. I have people working on it. While I appreciate your input, my captain is getting rather pointed with his comments about your participation in my cases. It's best if we take a break for a bit."

Maddie sighed and finished her coffee. "Very well. I will have to finish my work, then, instead of procrastinating. Though procrastinating is so very fun."

"We've all been working hard lately," Mike said. He took Maddie's empty cup and washed it out.

Maddie smiled. She loved to cook but hated the cleanup. Mike disliked the cooking but found it calming to wash up. Together, it made for quite the enjoyable partnership. They worked together well in many ways; it was why they often paired up for their freelance ghostwriting.

In her opinion, a great friendship was always the basis for a great partnership.

"How tired are you?" Mike asked as he turned back to the two of them.

"Tired enough not to feel like doing anything," Carson replied. "Not tired enough to sleep. I have work, though."

"You can blow work off," Mike wheedled.

Maddie wrinkled her nose. "I'm not tired at all. I want to do something and break from the daily grind of life. Let's go to Hawaii."

Carson chuckled. "I don't think that's possible for me at the time being."

"Nor I," Mike said, but he was grinning. "Let's go around town looking at the snowmen, shall we? I have new neighbors in the cul-de-sac, and I would love to confuse them as to what sort of relationships I have. What do the two of you say?"

"I say that I will have to leave you to your drama-stirring," Carson said with a laugh. "I only stopped in because I wanted to let you both know I'll be busy the next few days. I need to head into the office."

Mike opened his mouth as though to argue, but Maddie cut in. "And we would not want to jeopardize your job. After all, you are the best detective in the precinct."

She appreciated having Carson in her life, but there were still a few things she wanted to talk to Mike alone about before bringing them to Carson's attention. She gave him a pointed look.

Carson returned the look. He understood her well, and Maddie knew he was picking up on her energy. "No, I wouldn't want to jeopardize anything. You both take lots of pictures of the snowmen, though. We can have our own judging party for them tonight at my place."

"Thank you," Maddie said. "Give me fifteen minutes, and I'll be ready to head out, Mike."

Mike wiped the crumbs off the table into his palm. "All right. Just remember to bring your notebook. Who knows, we might see or think of something important."

CHAPTER 3

Maddie breathed the clean-scented air deeply. As much as she despised being cold in any shape, way, or form, there was still something peaceful and beautiful about this time of year. Everything was blanketed in fresh snow, a blank slate to write omens of the future.

She smiled to herself. It was a line from a story she had written when she was in elementary school and remained one of her favorite things she had ever written.

"You want to talk about work or have a complete mental break?" Mike asked next to her.

Unlike her, with two knitted caps, a scarf, and puffy ski pants paired with a parka, Mike wore a simple overcoat. It was unbuttoned down, and his scarf was hanging loose around his neck. Maddie wanted to be jealous of him, but he had warned her she was wearing too much for the day's temperature, and he was right.

So, naturally, she couldn't admit that even to herself, not for winter weather.

"Nothing about work at all," Maddie said fervently. "The last thing I want is to feel guilty that I'm enjoying this sunlight instead of being cooped up in my office, staring at a blank screen while I beat myself up for not having thoughts in my head."

Mike looped an arm around her shoulders as he laughed. "Ah, *mon Cheri*—I mean, *ma Cherie*," he corrected himself.

Maddie smiled. It had only taken him years to figure out that *mon* was the masculine form and *ma* the feminine. His name might be French, but he didn't learn the language.

"*Ma Cherie*," Mike started again, "I vould not vant you to beat yourself up."

"Is that supposed to be a French accent? It sounds more German," Maddie teased.

Mike shrugged. "So, this case that Carson is stuck on. What do you think? Is the man dead or just in hiding?"

They rounded the corner into the cul-de-sac Mike lived in. Every house on the street, besides Mike's, had a snowman in the front yard. Some of them were pretty elaborate, too. Maddie enjoyed looking at them as she considered Mike's question.

"As much as I don't condone what he did, I hope he's alive."

"Oh?"

Maddie stopped and stared at him. "Did you think I'd hope he was dead?"

Mike shook his head, holding his bare hands to the sunny air. "No, no. That's not what I mean at all. I was just wondering why it was. If you have any reasons besides decent people rarely wish death on others."

"I'm thinking of his children. Even if he wasn't the best of fathers, he was their primary caretaker for many years. I can't imagine how hard it would be for that person to die suddenly."

"But given what we know of him, there's a possibility he was abusive."

Maddie started walking again. "The possibility, yes. And if that is the case, they will be better off without that abuse in their lives. All the same, if I were in their position, I would rather my father be removed from my life in ways other than death."

"I suppose."

"I don't want to talk about this anymore," Maddie said briskly. "Let's admire these snowmen. Even your new neighbors have gotten into the spirit… although their snowman-making skills leave something to be desired."

She observed the massive mound of snow in their yard. While everyone else had lovingly shaped theirs into these perfectly round balls set one on top of each other, these neighbors had what appeared to be a sausage of snow standing straight up. Some work had been done to give it shape, but not much. It was even leaning to one side, propped up by a stepladder.

"It looks rather ugly, doesn't it?" Mike mused. "Maybe they're going for a Frankenstein theme?"

As they drew closer, Maddie noted that the hat on top of the snowman looked like it had come out of a trash bin. The scarf around its neck was full of moth holes, and a pair of snow boots stuck awkwardly out on either side of the thing.

It was all such a strange-looking thing that she couldn't help but giggle at the sight. The house was beautiful, and she knew it hadn't sold for cheap—she had considered buying it herself and moving out of the apartment. The back had the most enormous yard in the cul-de-sac, with this beautiful pergola the previous neighbors always strung with lights throughout winter.

So why did a family who could afford to buy such a house not be able to afford decent-looking accessories for their snowman?

She giggled again but attempted to swallow it down. She didn't want her first interaction with this family to be rude. Perhaps the decorations had sentimental value?

Mike rapped sharply on the door once they were on the front step. Footsteps echoed inside the house, and soon a tall, balding man answered. He had large, pale eyes and a red nose. With his full beard and the red shirt he wore, Maddie could have mistaken him for Santa Claus.

"Hello," Mike said brightly, holding out his hand. "Mike Malison here. I live in the greenhouse across the street. This here is Maddie, my friend."

"Hello," Maddie said with a polite nod.

The Santa Claus man smiled, though it appeared somewhat strained. "Henry Silver. It's a really friendly neighborhood here. My wife, Christine, and I have hardly had time to unpack with everyone coming over to say hello."

Maddie thought he was trying to make a point with that, but since Mike had said he wanted to leave them wondering about his relationships, she smiled brightly. "Oh, I know how that is! When I moved into my apartment, there were so many visitors all the time. People kept coming by and bringing me casseroles or pies. Of course, I want to offer the same to you and your wife, but I need to know if you have any allergies, how many people are in the house, and all that."

Henry seemed intrigued at the mention of food. "No, no allergies. It's just Christine and me here. But you don't have to make anything."

"It's no trouble. I'll whip up my special pumpkin pie for you." Maddie smiled again. She had never made pumpkin pie, but how hard could it be?

This is much better than trying to work on writing, she thought.

"Really," Henry started, but Mike interrupted.

"I will have to have you two come over some time. Do you like brandy? I have this excellent bottle of brandy."

"Henry," a voice called from inside the house. "Who is it?"

Henry sighed as though he had just been caught with a hand in the cookie jar. "Neighbors, dear."

A flurry of footsteps answered, and within a few seconds, a short, round woman with grey hair pulled into a knot at the top of her head was squeezing past Henry. Her cherry cheeks glowed as she clapped her hands. "Oh, visitors! How lovely. Please, please, come in."

Henry looked rankled, and it occurred to Maddie that this was exactly why he had been so short with them earlier. She felt a little bad at playing the overly friendly neighbor, but on the other hand, she loved getting into a role.

"Thank you so much," she gushed as she entered the house.

Mike made a discontented noise and followed her in.

"My, what a lovely end table," Maddie said, admiring the dark wood.

Really, it was the only thing there was to admire. Oddly, a grey-haired couple like this should have a lifetime's worth of furniture and momentums to fill a house like this. But there weren't even pictures on the walls.

"Thank you," Christine said. She wiped imaginary dust off the top of it. "I'm sorry I can't offer you anywhere to sit so we can talk. The movers have been an absolute nightmare. They said they would have brought our stuff in from the old house by now but do you see anything?"

She spread her arms out and shook her head in disgust.

Maddie nodded sympathetically. "Isn't it just awful how service workers pretend to work these days? Why, when I moved a piano into my apartment, they said they would be there at noon on the dot. They didn't even call me, I called them the next day, and it was still a week before I got that piano."

Christine clucked her tongue as she folded her arms. "Here I thought this town would be better than Spokane. At least the neighbors are friendly. And there's this delightful snowman contest."

By this time, Henry had slunk off somewhere, probably the kitchen or office. It seemed he didn't like to have visitors like his wife did.

"Yes, this snowman contest is wonderful," Mike agreed. "I haven't taken the time to put mine out yet, but I'm hoping to do so soon here."

Christine turned to Maddie. "And what about you, dear? Are you participating, or are there some rules against it at your apartment building?"

"Oh, I don't make snowmen. I don't like being cold," Maddie said. "I love yours, though. He looks so unique."

Christine laughed. "Oh, that thing? We're not done it yet. Henry's got this big plan in his skull about what he wants to happen with it, but he needs more equipment before it's finished. I threw on that old scarf and hat to trick the neighbors."

Mike winked at her. "Is it a trick when you tell the neighbors what's what?"

"Perhaps."

Maddie laughed. "I think it's a good joke."

"Thank you, Dear. Now, Henry and I are going to throw a little backyard party tomorrow. We just love that pergola, and it will be perfect for a wintertime barbeque." Christine smiled at the both of them. "I would love for you two to come."

"We'll be there," Mike said before Maddie could make up an excuse why she couldn't.

"Excellent!" Christine beamed at them, and Maddie didn't have the heart to say she wouldn't attend.

Ah, well. Perhaps a winter barbeque would be nice—if they didn't all freeze to death, that was.

CHAPTER 4

Mike would have enjoyed spending the whole day wandering around the town and playing distinct characters. Once they escaped from the Silver's new house, however, Maddie suggested they return to her apartment to get work done. Given how much work the two of them had to do, Mike reluctantly agreed.

They worked quickly after that, though, and got several days' worth of work done in that single afternoon, completing the project. Mike decided they would celebrate by ordering Chinese food and bingeing *The Witcher* until they fell asleep. Maddie happily agreed.

"Sometime I want to try my hand at Chinese dishes," she said as she bundled up for the walk to his house. "Authentic stuff. Maybe I should learn Mandarin and Cantonese to tour China and learn from chefs there."

"No, don't do that," Mike protested at once. Maddie gave him a shocked look, and, knowing he had one chance to claw this back, he gave her an exaggeratedly sad face. "I'd *miss* you."

"You could come with me."

"Carson would miss us."

Maddie laughed as she shoved her feet into boots. "If you're worried about him, we should invite him to dinner. You've been obsessing over this Ned Vande case all day, anyway."

"I have not."

"Have too."

"Have not."

Maddie bumped Mike with her shoulder, giggling. "Oh, so we're being immature today, are we?"

"Can't be mature with a fried brain," Mike grinned back at her, but it was to cover up the sudden knot in his stomach.

Between what Maddie had said this morning and all the hints she had been dropping throughout the day, he was worried that she was getting ready to pull up stakes here. He'd gotten very comfortable with the rhythm of their work, their partnership with ghostwriting and self-publishing.

He wasn't sure how difficult it would become to continue if he didn't have her excitement to fall back on. And worse, if she moved away, Coeur D'Alene might end up drab and boring. He loved this place. He loved being on the edge of the giant lake and being so close to places like Spokane and far enough away that he didn't feel suffocated by the city.

But what he really liked was having such close friends. Yes, he'd stay a good friend to Carson, but it wouldn't be the same without Maddie around.

He cleared his throat, shaking off those thoughts. Maybe it would be best to have Carson join them tonight, after all. It meant Maddie would avoid talking about all this moving stuff, at least.

He sent Carson a text and got one in reply, agreeing to the plan.

"You ever get the feeling that he only tags along with these sorts of things because he's worried we'll end up hurting ourselves?" Maddie asked once they were headed out of the apartment.

"Huh? No, I think he enjoys hanging out with us. It gives him that parental feeling without feeling responsible," Mike shrugged.

"I suppose, yeah."

She was quiet as they walked to the cul-de-sac. Carson was already waiting for them in his police cruiser. Even though he was a detective, the department was having a hard time with vehicles, and for the time being, Carson had to use the white car with *Coeur D'Alene Police Department* written along the side.

Snow was falling at this time, and Maddie had buried herself deep in the layers of her snow gear. They entered Mike's house while greeting each other, and Maddie made straight for his electric fireplace and turned it on.

"I don't know why you accepted that invitation to go to the Silvers' winter barbeque," she complained to Mike while he put away his snow stuff. She was still fully wrapped up. "I'm going to freeze to death."

"What's this? A winter barbeque?" Carson asked, one of his brows arched.

"Yeah. We can talk about it as we wait for the food," Mike said.

He headed into the kitchen, grabbed the menu of his favorite Chinese place in town, and then selected an appropriate wine-like beverage from his fridge. Wine-like because he liked to tease Maddie with the cheapest stuff. She knew where he kept the superb wine.

She didn't even make a face today when he set the wine-drink on the table. Though that could be because she was so focused on holding her fingers against the heat blower in the electric fireplace.

"Should I order the usual, or does anyone want something new?" Mike asked, pulling out his phone.

"Usual is good for me," Carson said.

Maddie hummed. "I want something new. Let's add some of that steam-fish roe and maybe the chicken feet."

Mike shared a startled look with Carson. Those were both options that, in the past, she had been adamant about not trying. *I know it's because I grew up in the blandest part of Vancouver, but I don't think I could eat anything if I had to look at the feet of any animal.*

"Are you feeling okay?" Carson asked in concern.

Maddie turned, a puzzled look on her face. "What? I think we need to try something new."

"Are you sure about the chicken feet?" Mike asked cautiously.

"I've been thinking about getting into some cooking school or taking a job in a kitchen somewhere as a break. The creative well doesn't run dry, but sometimes I tire of pumping out the ideas,"

Maddie said with a shake of her head. She finally took off her winter clothes when she spied the bottle on the table. "Ugh. Really? I know you still have that bottle I bought for you last week."

Mike picked up the wine-drink and waved it in her face. "But what happened to trying something new?"

Maddie opened her mouth, looking like she was about to argue, but then laughed. It was the brightest, most real laugh she'd given all week. "You're right! I shouldn't be such a snob. Chicken feet and wine to drink it is!"

At least the mood had lightened. Mike quickly ordered their food and got the glasses and utensils they needed. Carson cleared his throat as they all settled down to wait for the delivery.

"Now that we have that figured out. What's this about a barbeque at the Silvers' house?" His expression was neutral. Mike knew what that meant. He was brooding over something he didn't want to worry Maddie and Mike about.

"We stopped over to see them," Mike said. "They just moved into the cul-de-sac. They said they were having a party tomorrow in the pergola, and I accepted their invitation."

Carson frowned as he leaned forward. "Make up a reason to break that invitation."

Startled, Mike glanced at Maddie. She looked just as surprised. Carson rarely acted like this.

"Why?" Mike asked.

Carson pulled his hands over his face as though he was struggling with himself. Eventually, he shook his head. "I suppose the only option is to tell you. I believe Ned Vande was murdered, and Henry and Christine Silver are both suspects."

Mike nearly laughed out loud. As it was, he made a strangled sort of snorting noise. How could those grey-haired people be killers? He had seen images of Ned Vande. He was a tall, muscular man who had played football for almost a decade before an injury took him out of the game. Even Henry wasn't burly enough to take on a man like that.

"But they look like Santa and Mrs. Claus," Maddie protested.

"I know but looks can be deceiving." Carson picked up the wine-drink bottle and poured them each a cup. His dark expression slowly lightened, and he was chuckling when he set the bottle back down and handed out the drinks.

Maddie, sitting curled up in her favorite chair, frowned at him. As usual, she wore an oversized knitted sweater. The neck was too large and slipped off her shoulder as she took her drink. "What's funny?"

"Just this morning, I told you I would not involve you in this case, and less than a day later, suddenly, I'm telling you everything."

"You haven't told us anything yet," Mike pointed out. He leaned back on the couch and crossed his legs. "So. How are the Silvers connected to Ned Vande, and how could Santa Claus have killed the TikTok star?"

Carson sipped his drink and winced. Mike wasn't sure if it was the case or the taste he was wincing at. He waited, feeling himself edging closer to the edge of his seat with each passing second.

"First, you know that Ned Vande wasn't just cheating and lying to his viewers about what he did," Carson finally said, just as Mike thought he was about to fly apart at the seams.

"Oh?" Maddie pushed, yet somehow sounded polite about it. She had such an elegant aura around her.

"He has been under investigation by the IRS for some time," Carson continued. "It looked as though he might get money under the table. As it turned out, they were right... Ned Vande bought his internet popularity. The vast majority of his first influx of followers were bot accounts, and with them, he gamed the algorithm to end up everywhere."

Mike had to admit he was actually impressed by that.

"How did he get that money?" Maddie asked. "From what I know, he got laid off from his job, and he and his wife were struggling for money. That's why he started the channel."

Carson shook his head. "Smuggling."

Maddie's eyes widened. "You mean like that diamond smuggling case we solved last year? Was he involved in that?"

"It seems he might be, but I don't have any evidence for it, which brings me to the Silvers. I've looked into them, and I found they have been charged a dozen times for involvement in smuggling. Gems, drugs, black market artifacts. They've been doing this for decades all across the country. But nothing has stuck."

Mike thought of the hallway table in the Silver's house. Was it some ancient, rare antique? It looked like something that you could buy at Walmart. "Not enough evidence?"

"You could say that." Carson's gaze darkened. "Seems they're good at getting rid of the evidence."

"Oh, no," Maddie breathed. "You mean… witnesses?"

"That's exactly what I mean," Carson said grimly.

Mike leaned back, a chill settling over them. They seemed to be such charming, grandparent-like people! It just went to show you couldn't trust your eyes in these matters. He sucked on his teeth as he considered the situation.

"And you think Ned Vande was one of these witnesses?" Maddie asked.

Carson's expression only grew more serious. "Yes."

CHAPTER 5

The three of them sat in silence. It was undoubtedly a grim outlook for sure; a missing man, known criminals in their midst. He imagined it would be even more shocking for his two young companions. After all, he had been careful not to reveal too much earlier since it would cause problems with the Captain if they had to give the credit for another solved case to civilians.

Mike finally finished his drink and set the empty glass down. "So, Ned Vande was involved in the Silvers' smuggling organization, and with the IRS sniffing around, they ended him rather than take the chance he'd squeal?"

"That's what it looks like," Carson agreed.

A ring came at the doorbell, announcing their food. Mike headed over to answer it, and Carson poured himself another drink. This beverage tasted nothing like wine. It was far too sweet. So sweet, in fact, that he couldn't taste the alcohol. Which meant he would need to be very careful with it.

"Here we go," Mike said as he returned. He set the boxes on the coffee table and handed Carson and Maddie their chopsticks. He settled back on the couch and grabbed an empty plate to pick himself up. "All right. The Silvers moved in a month ago."

"A month and they still have nothing in their house except this cheap end table in their entrance hallway," Maddie said, picking out a fish-and-roe ball and a chicken foot.

Carson took a few chicken feet himself. He had always loved these dishes; they reminded him of his first girlfriend's house. Of course, the taste was never quite the same, but the memories were good. "Do you think they could hide anything on the table?"

"I wondered if it might be an antique," Mike said.

Maddie shook her head. "No way. They got that thing from a thrift shop for ten bucks; I guarantee it. However, I noticed some scratches where the legs connect to the table. If they've changed it, they might use it for smuggling."

"Which is the FBI's jurisdiction—not that they listen to anything us detectives have to say." Carson attempted to keep his expression smooth.

He couldn't say he was surprised that the agents he'd talked to had completely dismissed his concerns. After all, this was hardly a central hub for the crime. He grunted as he speared a piece of broccoli with his chopsticks.

Mike toyed with his food. "There's that snowman, too."

"Snowman?" Maddie and Carson both repeated.

The two glanced at each other. Mike did things like this from time to time, talking about things that didn't seem relevant at all but often would open up the case to what really happened. It didn't solve things all the time, but it did often enough that it earned him a bit of grace.

"The snowman on the Silvers' yard. I knew it was strange. I think I just figured out why." Mike grinned and shoveled food into his mouth.

"Don't do that," Maddie complained.

Mike moved his food into a cheek. "Do what?"

Carson answered. "Don't be dramatic. Just tell us what you figured out about that snowman."

"It's not normal, is it?" Mike said.

"Finish your mouthful, then talk," Maddie ordered, looking faintly nauseated. She nibbled on the chicken foot, and Carson wasn't sure if it was her preconceived notions of the meal or Mike's full mouth giving her that expression.

Mike obliged, and after he'd wiped his mouth with a napkin, he leaned forward. "The snowman that the Silvers have in their front yard. It looks more like they've rolled snow around something and packed in the open parts that tried to make an actual snowman."

"Christine said they were planning on fixing it up," Maddie said doubtfully. She shook her head and continued even as Mike grinned. "But if their house is so empty after a month, they can't plan to stick around, so why would they even care about the contest? I feel Christine was just talking about the things that seemed off to answer our unasked questions."

Carson didn't like the sound of that. "Before we get further, I would prefer the two of you stay in Maddie's apartment or stay at my place tonight. The Silvers will have seen the cruiser outside, and I don't want them to decide you two are a threat."

Mike waved a hand at him. "We'll figure that out later. Back to the snowman."

"The snowman," Maddie repeated, sounding a little sarcastic. "The all-important snowman."

"They put it up before the contest was announced." Mike paused and looked between Maddie and Carson for his dramatic effect.

Carson couldn't help but feel an exasperated fondness well over him. "When did they put it up?" he pressed.

"About a week ago."

Maddie straightened. "Wait! What are you saying? You think—"

"Ned Vande is in the snowman?" Mike nodded. "I do. Mrs. Fenning was complaining about it a week ago. She told me they woke her up at three in the morning with a truck pulling into the cul-de-sac, and Henry Silver rolled a big pillar of snow out of the back."

Carson lowered his plate. The thought of a man being stuck in that snowman was grisly, but the temperatures had been well below freezing for some time. With the added insulation of the snow, it was unlikely that a corpse would thaw out enough to attract predators.

"Why didn't you say anything before now?" he demanded.

"I had nothing to base it on."

Carson bit back a sigh. Of course not. Carson himself had only learned the Silvers were involved in illegal activity recently, and his

Captain had told him not to let Mike and Maddie know about it this time. It seemed to be a safe enough option until he learned the two had been invited into their house!

Catching his eye, Mike shook his head. "Until now, I thought they were just a couple of retired folks who moved into town and were busy visiting family as they set up. I would never have pegged them for criminals, let alone murderers."

"And that's exactly how they keep getting away with it," Carson said grimly.

He pulled his cell phone from his pocket. The Captain would not be happy to have his dinner interrupted, but if they could solve a missing person's case and bring in two criminals that the FBI was after? It would be enough for him to overlook any annoyance at Carson.

"I have to report this," he said. "Before I investigate."

"It's out in the open; can't you just knock it over and see what falls out?" Maddie asked.

Carson shook his head. "It's on private property, and with how rich the Silvers are from all their illegal activity, they can hire a slick lawyer. I don't want them to get off free because of some technicality."

"What if one of us knocked it over, then?" Mike suggested.

"Out of the question." Carson sent a text to the Captain, explaining that he may have just cracked the case.

Mike began eating again, but it was Maddie who frowned. "Why not? We could drink, so we're actually drunk, and go around knocking over all the snowmen. Then the Silvers won't know that we did it on purpose."

"It's too dangerous," Carson insisted.

His phone dinged. The Captain had responded, telling him to wait until the next day. Carson had to roll his eyes. While he had great respect for the old Captain, things had been getting sloppy in the precinct of late.

He stood and walked to the next room before calling his Captain.

He was greeted with, "Luttrell, I told you this would wait until tomorrow."

"It can't," Carson replied, keeping his voice level and flat. "I believe that I have found Ned Vande, Sir. Get me a warrant, and I'll prove it. It will be a good boost for the precinct," he added.

He wasn't up on TikTok and other social media platforms, but apparently, a big fuss was happening over this disappearance. They had had protestors camped outside the building for a few days even, though only a few, and they left as soon as they were confronted.

There was still the narrative making its rounds that the police were ignoring the case because Ned had been a stay-at-home dad, in any case. Some people just didn't want to accept that was a false persona that he'd presented to them.

"Bah. It can wait—"

"And if I'm right about who killed them, we'll have one up on the FBI," he added.

The Captain was quiet for a moment, then, "What do you need?"

Carson grinned.

CHAPTER 6

Mike put his plate of food on the coffee table. His sense of triumph at figuring out the case faded as he looked at Maddie. Everything she'd been talking about and hinting at returned to him in a rush.

"Maddie, can I ask you something personal?" he asked, feeling oddly nervous, which was strange. He could talk to Maddie and Carson about anything. They were the only two people in the world he was this comfortable with.

"Yes, you can use this in your next story," Maddie replied.

Mike managed a small smile. "That's not what I meant. I meant personal about you."

"Oh. Personal how?"

Mike hesitated. "You haven't been yourself lately, and all this talk about wanting to do new things... it's got me a little concerned. Are you happy?"

Maddie blinked at him, the freckles on her nose making a little constellation of stars as she scrunched it up, deep in thought. "Yes. I'm happy."

"But you also feel stuck?"

"I feel... like I should do more with my life. Maybe I'm feeling burnt out. Maybe I'm feeling like life is repetitive right now, and I want a break from the ordinary to start appreciating the ordinary again." She nibbled on a piece of ginger beef. "Maybe I need to expand my horizons."

Mike held his breath, looking for the right words, but the question burst out of him in a rush before he could think things through. "Are you doing to move away?"

Maddie's hazel eyes widened. "Move away? No! I love it here. Snow and all. I'm not moving anywhere. I was thinking about something like revamping my resume and getting a job at a restaurant or a bakery or something."

Relief washed over him as he slumped back on his couch. Suddenly all the worries he'd been trying to avoid all day seemed so silly he could have laughed at himself. What a thing to fret over when it wasn't even on Maddie's mind!

"I think that's a great idea," he said. "You've always been clever at cooking and baking and switching things up sometimes is always good."

Maddie smiled back at him. "You will not discourage me? We've been doing so much work together lately…."

"Maddie, I will never discourage you from trying new angles in life," Mike assured her. "And you know what else? If you want to talk about anything, just let me know. I'm here for you. Whether that's jobs or romance or children. I'm here."

Maddie put her plate down and got to her feet. She rounded the table and pulled Mike into a tight hug. "Thank you. I am thinking about fostering, but not now. I will not make that sort of commitment unless it's because I want to help the kids out. Not because I want to feel better about myself."

Mike hugged her back. "Of course, *ma Cherie*."

He kissed the top of her head and broke the hug, smiling at her.

The moment was broken by the sound of an engine starting outside. Under normal circumstances, it wouldn't have caught Mike's attention at all. Something about it tonight made the hairs on his arms stand on end.

His dark eyes met Maddie's hazel-green ones, and they both rushed to the front door at the same time.

A giant moving van stood outside of the Silvers' house. Mike's heart jumped to his throat. No! They were going to move the body, and then the truth of what happened to Ned Vande would vanish forever. Whatever criminal activity they had gotten him twisted up in would continue. How long before they were stopped?

How many more bodies?

"Get Carson," he said, his voice tense.

Maddie turned on her heel and rushed away. Something big moved on the other back side of the moving van, and a little voice worried that he was being foolish. But in the face of everything he had learned within the last few hours, he knew he couldn't let them get away with this.

He was out of the door before thinking of the implications of stopping himself. His bare feet kicked through the snow as he drove across the yard, heading toward the moving van and the two people on the other side.

"Help!" he yelled the first thing that came to mind, the only reason he'd be dashing out without even putting on his shoes. "Call 9-1-1! He's going to kill her!"

The massive pillar of snow containing Ned Vande dropped as Henry and Christine cried out. A dolly fell in the other direction, falling onto Henry's foot. He started hopping on his other foot, letting out a stream of pained curses.

"What are you talking about?" Christine demanded, grabbing Mike's arm. "Who's killing who?"

"The cop," Mike yelled.

Henry waved a hand at him. "Be quiet! You'll wake the neighbors!"

Oh. What a good idea! Mike almost grinned. "HELP!" he yelled louder than ever. "SOMEONE PLEASE HELP!"

"Mike!" Carson's voice came from behind them. He turned to see the detective rushing across the road.

"It's him!" Mike shouted. Carson would understand; they'd worked together often enough for him to catch on. At least, Mike hoped he would as he hid behind Henry and Christine. He raised his voice even louder. "He tried to kill Maddie!"

Carson came up short as the older couple looked at him bewilderedly. His eyes flickered to Mike, but just as Mike guessed, he knew what role to play.

"Mike don't be silly," Carson said, lifting his hands in a placating gesture. "You don't know what you saw."

Mike backed away from the Silvers toward their fallen snowman. Warrant or no warrant, he couldn't let them get away! "I saw everything. I saw you... and her... stay away! Oh, someone, please help! He'll kill me too."

"I don't know what's going on here, but I demand you both leave at once," Henry snarled.

Mike couldn't understand how Maddie thought he looked like Santa Claus. He ignored the Silvers as he backed slowly up. His legs hit the snowman, and he took a deep breath, then nodded once at Carson.

"Mike, let's go back to your home and talk about this," Carson said, creeping forward.

"No! You'll kill me too!" Mike threw himself back, knocking into the snowman.

Henry shouted.

Christine yelled.

And the wail of sirens rose in the distance.

* ✳ ❄ ✳ *

The next day, Mike, Maddie, and Carson met again at Maddie's apartment. Mike sneezed into his mug of hot cocoa as Carson brought a small bottle of cold medicine and put it on the table beside him.

"Running after two known murderers like that was foolish," he said.

"I didn't know that you already had people on the way," Mike protested. His feet were still cold from his 'adventure.' "All I knew was that they loaded that snowman up and would take him away, and we'd never learn the truth."

"We would have caught them," Carson said.

Maddie settled into her chair again, holding a cup of tea. "Perhaps. But they had time to split before the other police showed up, and if they had gotten to the highway, it would have been difficult to catch them before they dumped the body. I think Mike was fearless."

"Perhaps," Carson admitted. A smile tugged at his lips.

Sipping his coco, Mike fixed Carson with a stare. "Well? Don't hold us in suspense. What happened with the Silvers? Was Ned Vande in that snowman?"

"He was," Carson said. He settled on the couch. "And you were right hallway table. The legs had been hollowed out and filled with emeralds. The Silvers have confessed to it all in exchange for a prison sentence they can serve together. They had Vande smuggle in gems for them, and he used the excuse of being a TikTok star to get to places most people wouldn't."

Mike nodded. They had already figured that part out.

"When they learned he was in trouble with the IRS, they realized it was only a matter of time before he squealed. They leaked the information about him lying to his fans and cheating on his wife," Carson continued. "And when enough time had passed for things to get worse for him, they offered him a place to hide out. Once he was there, they killed him."

"And then put him in that snowman," Maddie concluded.

Carson nodded.

Mike sneezed again. "At least it's over," he said. "Although I'm disappointed that we've had this heat wave. All the snowmen have melted before the contest."

"Which reminds me...." Maddie grabbed a bag beside her chair and handed it to him. "For you."

Mike set his coco aside and took the bag, puzzled. He opened it up and stared. He held a small white figure in his hand. It had the shape of a woman, painted in something that glittered slightly. It had a tiny felt hat glued to its head and an orange toothpick on its nose.

"And what is this?" he asked.

Maddie grinned. "It's no man. Like 'snowman.' It-sno-man."

"No," Carson groaned. "That was awful."

Mike grinned at her. A 'no man' to commemorate the winter. It was no snowman, but he had fresh memories with Carson and Maddie.

"Thank you," he said. "It's perfect."

The End

MURDER IN THE SNOW

A WILMA WADE HOLIDAY MYSTERY

CHAPTER 1

The moment Miss Wilma Wade steps into her home, she flinches at the sound of her footsteps echoing through the rooms. It's a small house. The walls are pressed forward like they are pleading to be saved. After spending a few days with her cousin who lives in Barwick, Maine, Wilma can't help but think there's always going to be something missing in her home.

Wilma used to like the quiet; she enjoyed it even. But her cousin Martha is not the sort of woman to keep quiet. As such, her Christmas holiday was filled with a lot of talk around the fireplace. Martha recently lost her husband, which is a terrible thing to think about. But on the day Wilma left, she took Wilma into her arms and brushed the grey hair from her face.

"Will you be all right?" Wilma had asked.

She shrugged. And then, just as Wilma had pulled away, she said, "My children will keep visiting. And the grandkids too."

Alone in her own home now, Wilma wants to call Martha. Of course, there won't be much to talk about except how her garden is now covered with snow, and how she can't step outside without digging her shoes into the snow. But Wilma yearns to hear Martha's voice come alive at the other end of the line.

She does not make the phone call, however. Wilma wants to become accustomed to the quiet again, reborn in her house's slow rebellion, watching it unfold around her. As she makes breakfast, Wilma's memories are off the walls in her kitchen, ricocheting straight toward her. She remembers her lover who died during the Desert Storm Conflict and how his eyes had brightened up her younger days. She'd promised herself she wouldn't give her heart to another when he died.

The memories are the only things she's got now. But even as they spiral out of control, she does not stop them. Instead, after a breakfast of undercooked rice and curry soup, Wilma goes into her living room and writes about it. Her writing is slow and pretentious. But she writes about his face that burns in her memory. She writes of his time on earth, dragging his last days with painful addiction. Later, about halfway through her story, Wilma feels an unexpected lucidity, like a secondhand thrill.

When she'd bought this house, a part of her had ached to become one with the architecture. It's strange, now, how distant it makes her feel. Wilma knows when nostalgia has hit, which is why she hates being away from her house; she has a faint idea of the happiness that exists in quiet homes and the cheap thrill of being awakened by loudness. Still, she does not regret spending the Christmas holiday with Martha. She misses it.

The week between Christmas and New Year has always been Wilma's favorite. That week, she gets the chance to spill words from her stories to strangers and not feel ridiculously small. The truth is, Wilma's not a woman who indulges in life's excesses. She has always been conservative. But in that one week, everything is different, and Wilma becomes another person entirely. It is always an eventful one for her, mainly because it's the only time she can gather her thoughts and not want to hide away.

Every year, Wilma has made this season like a festival at the General Hospital. Sometimes, she goes there with her books all stacked neatly in a small bag. Other times, she goes along with homemade cookies. The nurses tell her it's delicious, but Wilma does not believe such flattery. Still, it genuinely makes her happy to add these minor details.

This year, Wilma cannot go. When she climbs out of bed in the morning, she can surely tell she will not make it. She tiptoes downstairs, pulling her robe over her clothes. She's left her jackets underneath a pile of clothes against her better judgment. The robe is the only thing she can easily reach, and that's what she does. It's no justification, but Wilma is alone in her home. She tells herself it's fine as she goes into the living room.

The only place in her home welcomes her like it's always known her. Sometimes, Wilma thinks it knows her. She has once held on to the belief that her house has a soul. But not anymore. Still, her living room makes her feel welcome despite everything. When Wilma opens the curtain and peers outside, she gasps.

A vast sea of foam gathers around her, stretching its weak fingers over the space. She can't tell what she'd been dreaming about when the snow fell and buried the ground as far as her eyes can see. But she thinks it has got to be a peaceful dream, the sort where waking up feels problematic and sublime at the same time.

A blizzard has taken over the front of her house. And when Wilma stretches to see her neighbor's place, she sees the same picture, like a scene from an old movie. Wilma clutches her chest the minute her mind settles around the idea of shoveling the snow away. It's a chore she's still not used to because the cold makes it unbearable to do without feeling dizzy. But she does not think she can relax. With this much snow, there is no way Wilma can drive to General Hospital.

She wants to call them and break out an excuse, but something stops her. There, on her windowpane, is a frozen line resembling a tear. Wilma stares at the line, wondering how something so otherworldly can end up on her window while the front of her house is a mess. It makes her laugh, and as the laughter rolls off her tongue, it echoes in the silence. She stops herself suddenly and sighs.

She puts the kettle on the stove in her kitchen, readying herself for hot tea before shoveling snow. She is a seventy-year-old woman, and catching a cold is not on her list. Wilma waits until the kettle's whistling before turning the stove off and pouring the water into a cup. If Martha were here, she'd lean against the sink, one hand on her waist, the other on her chest. That's how she'd been after the funeral.

"What are you thinking?" Wilma had asked her.

"About my husband," she said. Understandable. Her husband had just been murdered. It was okay to think about him. Wilma is still thinking about her lover even after decades. "I don't think I can handle anything without him around."

Wilma had told her, "Of course you will. Just...don't overthink it."

Wilma is overthinking now about the snow in front of her house and the neighbor's place. She was thinking about the color of her tea turning a soft brown instead of the deep black she's always known. Perhaps it's spoilt? But when she checks the packet of tea, the expiration date is still a year away. Smoke sizzles upward away from the cup. She turns the liquid with a spoon and places it gently on the sink. Then, she takes a long sip and burns the tip of her tongue.

Wilma yelps and places the cup down. It's her own fault, she knows, because it's hard to control the urge to be powerful at all times. No, not powerful in that rash way of feeling immune to anything, but powerful enough to stay alive. With her burnt tongue, Wilma goes back to the window with the frozen line. It looks much like a crystal with the second gaze, and soon, Wilma forgets that she's burnt her tongue or left her tea unattended. Suddenly, it feels right to be there, by the window, watching the crystal ice. It has demarcated a part of her window now like the scratches of a witch. The line is growing, and Wilma likes it.

When she returns to her room, she settles for finding the right clothes for her morning chore before showering. She has always been like that: dissolving known patterns to fit into the small cravings of her mind. She finds an oversized jacket underneath the clothes and lays it out on the edge of her bed. Next, she scouts for pants and a sweater. And when she has everything laid out, she goes into the shower and lets the warm water envelop her skin.

Dressing up is not a hassle when she's laid out her clothes for the day. This time, the clothes are a fit for the coldness of the outside world. When she is done dressing up, Wilma returns to the window to look. The line has broken into two, like rivals racing for a win.

She makes a bet on the first line. It could win.

In the kitchen, she pours the cold tea away and makes breakfast: French and an overabundance of honey. She savors it, allowing her body to adjust to the food's sweetness. When it becomes soggy, she throws it away and marches to the window. The first line has broken.

And there is, in fact, a new winner. Wilma Wade is wrong, and she knows it.

CHAPTER 2

With a new winner, Wilma realizes two things: one, she is a lonely woman, and two, she's got a wild imagination. Both facts are as fundamental as anything she has ever known, and she does not turn them away when the thoughts come to her. It is just the way it is, she admits.

Once she opens the door of her house and steps outside, a chill runs up her body. Even with the sweater and jacket she has on, the cold meets her. She swallows and adjusts herself before going into the garage next to her house. She finds a snow shovel and a bag of sand and salt. She knows about the intricacies of being alone, which is why she always has these things handy. In her mind's eye, she can see how useful these things will be when she shovels the snowbank outside. On the pavement, when she is done, she will throw the salt and sand to make it a fine finish. That's what she thinks.

The first dip of her shovel in the snow makes her chuckle. Here, she finds that snow shoveling after a blizzard gets more challenging as she grows older, and it is this fragility that makes her want to cry, but Wilma ends up laughing until she's got tears threatening to fall. Another sweep through, and it gets easier. Though her arms are weakening as she shovels, she pushes on.

Her neighbors can't help her. Sometimes they help her while she makes hot tea and cheesecakes for them, but today is different. They go to spend the holidays with their grandparents and won't return until New Year's Eve. Today, she will have to do these things for herself. The more she rakes through the snow, the more it becomes routine. Of course, she is exhausted. But the more she does it, the more Wilma realizes she doesn't feel as lonely as before. Perhaps she's taking her house back into the skin of her hands. She isn't sure. But it feels good.

Two hours later, Wilma throws the snow shovel down, taking sharp breaths. It comes as a feeling, but after two hours of shoveling, Wilma thinks she's shoveled out almost everything. A second look again shows that she's made a good amount of progress, but she has not gotten to the street yet. Wilma has simply shoveled ten miles of sidewalks and another ten miles of driveways. As this realization creeps in, she grumbles. Her house is small, but the driveway is more than she can handle. It isn't like her to make a mistake. But now, Wilma isn't thinking about the interior of her house but about how she can maneuver her way around this pile of snow.

She is exhausted. In her upper hands, Wilma can barely feel anything. The wind has brushed against her cheeks too many times so that she now feels cracked. Exasperated, Wilma digs her snow shovel in again to rake out another batch when her shovel hits a hardened surface.

There is science in a pile of snow. Wilma has always believed that. When a person shovels too much of it and pauses, a chill envelops the person. Then, the snow becomes more rigid and stiffer like rocks. Wilma raises the shovel and tries again, but the hard surface is thicker and firmer. It couldn't be snow.

Standing there, her mind grapples with the idea that something may be hidden underneath the pile of snow. She can't overthink it, but Wilma is already frightened that she won't like what she'll find. Still, she pushes the snow around the surface, refusing to lift it since snow shoveling is a strenuous activity, and she is both tired and cold. Two minutes later, the surface clears off, and Wilma sees that the hardened surface is a frozen human.

The sudden change in the atmosphere has her gasping for air and tumbling backward. Somehow Wilma steadies herself before falling, planting her booted feet against the already shoveled path. Instinctively, she places one hand over her lips to keep herself from screaming, but when she looks down at the frozen body, she lets out a guttural shriek. There isn't anyone around, so Wilma stops screaming. Well, she has to be practical in such situations, right?

She goes back inside the house to find her phone. There are two missed calls from Martha and a voice message from the General Hospital. She makes a mental note to call Martha back and reply to the hospital message. But for now, there is something more pressing, to say the least.

In a cupboard, Wilma finds the hardcover book. There, she's stored countless phone numbers. With age, she has discovered that time passes quickly and so do the little things. Flipping through the pages, she sees the phone number of Detective Jason Fellow and starts dialing it. She is two decades older than he is, but often, she misses it when they speak. It isn't from his physical appearance; no. Detective Jason has a buzz cut that has gathered specks of gray. Still, he has got tight skin on his cheeks and arms. Sometimes, Wilma thinks he could be mistaken for a man in his mid-thirties.

He takes the call after the third ring, his voice raspy. "Good morning, Miss Wade. How's the holiday going over there?"

Wilma has no time or patience for small talk. "There is a dead person in my driveway."

Detective Jason sighs. "What were you doing outside, Miss Wade? It's freezing and let's not forget last night's blizzard."

"I was shoveling snow," she answers.

"You must be tired…"

She shakes her head vigorously but stops when she realizes he isn't listening. Her voice, this time around, is sharp. "I'm telling you, there's a frozen corpse on my driveway, Detective."

"Are you certain you aren't imagining things? Did you know that the cold sometimes makes room for hallucinations?"

Wilma does not know that; she can't be sure he isn't making it up on the spot. Still, a dead person is outside her house, and the feeling unsettles her.

"I am not imagining anything," she says. "It is cold outside, and there's snow everywhere, but there is also a body there."

Detective Fellow has known the old woman who has lived alone in her tiny house for some time. She is the woman who sometimes writes to read it at the General Hospital, and rarely has he heard her make anything up, especially matters concerning the police. Perhaps he ought to take her a little more seriously.

"Very well then," he says.

She hears him drag his breath, so she waits, one hand pressed firmly against the phone in her ear, for him to speak again.

He says, "I will send someone over to look around."

But Wilma wants him instead. She knows that if he doesn't take an issue as necessary, he won't come over himself; this is as important as anything can get. Wilma cracks her head for how to entice him until an idea brushes past her mind. Her eyes sparkle with mischievousness.

"I have some blueberries and French toast, Detective," she says to him. "What do you say you have them after taking care of the matter in front of my house? I have the best tea as well."

The silence at the other end of the line is deathly. Wilma can barely hear anything. When it seems unlikely he'll answer, she hangs up.

She redials and his voice comes back alive. "It must be the terrible network, Miss Wade, but I missed what you just said."

She told him again that the wait wasn't elevated this time. "Why! That's very good. All right, I will come and have a look. Sheriff Riley will accompany me as well. Let me tell you; we are always hungry in the morning after a blizzard."

Wilma says, "I'll have some servings ready for you. Thank you, Detective."

CHAPTER 3

Being inside the house alone makes Wilma overthink. So, despite the cold, she goes back outside and picks up her shovel. Her gloved hands finger the snow shovel handle while her eyes dart restlessly over the space. The sun is just settling in the sky above like fine specks of dust shimmering behind the clouds. In a matter of hours, Wilma is sure the sun will be warm, heavy, and capable of melting some of the snow.

Her dead visitor is still there, on the floor. She steps closer to him and sees that he is wearing pants and nothing more. His shirt is gone. On his torso, she sees light markings, almost like this dead man was beaten before his death. It makes her wonder if this death isn't just like the one she'd experienced back at Barwick.

When the two men arrive in a truck, they find Wilma, one hand over the shovel. Sheriff Riley maneuvers through the snow and parks the truck sideways.

"It's a new trick," he tells his partner. "This way, it becomes easy for us to pull out from the curb when it's time to go back."

But it is not a new trick. It is simply the most plausible thing to do in the situation. Detective Fellow is the first to climb out of the car but waits until Riley is by his side. Together, they walk forward, watching as Wilma leans against the shovel.

"Miss Wade?" Fellow says with an overenthusiastic tone. She recognizes the tone since she has heard it one too many times in the past.

"Detective," she greets him and then focuses her stare on the other man.

"Sheriff Riley," the man offers.

"Thank you for coming," she tells them and halts them with the wave of a palm. "Please don't come closer in this direction. The man is still here."

Sheriff Riley gives the Detective a knowing glance, and for a split second, Wilma thinks they are about to laugh in her face. Fellow looks worried, not about her, she understands, but for the body they can see sticking out of the snow. They step away from the straight path and come to meet her from the corner.

The Detective's feet are deep in snow when he speaks, "Well, your visitor is long dead."

She knows this already. That's what she's been telling him since she first made the call. Somehow, when she looks at the Detective, she thinks he means something else.

It is the Sheriff who gasps when his eyes fall on the body. By now, the sun is full, painting the horizon a feverish yellow.

"What could have happened here?" Sheriff asks, but it's rhetorical. Even Wilma knows that. "Could he have been a drunken fellow who'd lost his way home and fallen asleep here? Seems logical."

"Then how do you explain him shirtless?" Wilma asks.

Sheriff Riley bends over the body but does not touch it. "It's the holidays, Miss Wade. If he were really drunk, going shirtless in the snow would not have been that much of an issue."

Detective Fellow rubs his gloved hands together and sighs. "The markings tell of something different, Sheriff. Don't you think so?"

The Sheriff stands up and moves away from the body without another word. Perhaps he is conflicted with the entire situation or has a different conclusion, but he does not show it. She can't tell what he is thinking about.

Detective Fellow speaks, "Well, we should call Dr. McCall here before the poor man's body melts in the snow."

Wilma agrees immediately and takes the shovel back to the garage.

Detective Fellow and the Sheriff do not follow her into her house because of the dead man and how his body is positioned in the snow. From her window, she can see the men around the corpse, their hands on their waists and feet planted apart.

In her kitchen, Wilma rolls out the dough. She has already brought these men out in such cold conditions that it might seem terrible if she does not offer them something warm to eat. A few minutes later, Wilma sees an ambulance and a few cars stop in front of her house. Her hands pause around the rolling pin, her fingers crusted with the dough. She is thinking of making blueberry muffins as they move around the body.

A man in a doctor's uniform bends over the body and starts touching it. The group talks about the body and the snow. Wilma can hear muffles from their conversations. When Wilma puts the tray into the oven, she relaxes her shoulders and hands and steps outside. Wilma does not leave the porch even though the situation close to the body is ridiculously dipped in uncertainty. When the body is moved and put in a body bag, she sighs deeply and watches as they put it in the ambulance.

The clearing of the snow outside her home begins shortly. She is grateful for the help, really, but sad about the dead man and the weight of the snow. Her blueberry muffins are ready by now, so she returns and takes them out of the oven. They are covered in a fine brown that makes her giddy with exhaustion. Next, she places the kettle on the stove.

After a short while, only Sheriff Riley and Detective Fellow remain. When they knock on her door, and she opens it and leads them in, she sees that her entire front yard has been cleared off. She thanks them with palms pressed forward like an answer to a prayer.

"It's not a problem," Fellow tells her.

She lets them sit around her dining table while she brings in the tray of muffins. The tea is warm, and as she places the cups in front of the men; they see steam slithering upward.

A first bite and Riley says, "This is very good, Miss Wade. Thank you for the kind gesture."

She places one hand over her chest. "Well, of course, I should do this. I'm grateful you both could do something about the body. Poor soul."

When they are done eating, Riley offers to clear the table, despite Wilma's polite protests. Alone with the Detective, Wilma knits her fingers in front of her. Fellow makes no move to speak. And when she stares him down, Wilma can see that he is just as perplexed as she is about the entire case. She is not trained as they are, but Wilma is confident her mind is just as composed.

She tells him, "I am sorry I can't identify the body. Don't you find it strange that a man would die in front of my house?"

Sheriff Riley comes back and sits back on his chair. She thanks him before making eye contact with the Detective, speaking as though she never stopped. "I have just returned from a holiday with my cousin who lives in Barwick, Maine. I am afraid I couldn't tell you what this man's business was."

Detective Fellow shakes his head and opens his mouth to speak but pauses. This woman isn't a police officer, so Fellow can't be sure if it is telling her the right thing to do. Still, she is the woman who has helped him before in countless other cases. For a woman her age, Fellow thinks her brilliance is extraordinary.

"The thing is, according to Dr. McCall, the body looks old," Fellow tells her.

She swallows. "No, but the man looked young to me."

He waves her off with a hand. "I don't mean old as in his age, of course not. I mean, the corpse is old. It's been a while since he died."

"But... but when I returned to town a few days ago, I could still see the ground outside my home. There wasn't a dead body here."

"Then that could only mean one thing," Detective Fellow pauses and raises one hand above his head. The tension is high in the room, but even he is uncertain about what to do with the entire situation.

"What is it, Detective?" she throws the question at him because she is not the type to be kept in the dark. Wilma is curious, but more than that, she hates that someone could have done this deliberately.

"The man died somewhere else and was brought here to make it seem like he was frozen under last night's blizzard," Fellow proposes.

Wilma says, "Clearly, that would have failed either way since the police and the forensics team would have tested the body. That's part of their jobs, right?"

This time, Sheriff Riley chirps in dutifully. "I don't think whoever put the body here cared for any of that. It didn't matter if the body was found, obviously. I think whoever put the body here did it for fun or to push the blame on you."

Wilma shakes her head and bites down hard against her lower lips. "Do you mean a criminal brought a dead man to my front door just for fun? That's unbelievable."

Some things are relatively easy to understand and believe, but this is far from that. Wilma feels nauseous as she speaks, but it is not something that can be helped, considering the entire situation.

"We'll find out soon enough," Detective Fellow says. "The body has been taken away, and soon, we expect to hear from Dr. McCall."

Wilma shuffles her feet underneath the table and says, "What about his identity? Do you know the victim?"

"It's still the early days," Fellow answers. "In a matter of hours, we'll be able to know his identity, Miss Wade."

Wilma says nothing for a long time, and before long, the silence has become razor-thin, slicing through the air. Finally, when a thought crosses her mind, Wilma leans forward. "So, what can I do? Do I have to wait until another body is found outside my home again?"

That is a line the Detective and the Sheriff have not thought of before. If the culprit left the body in front of her house as a sick joke on her age, then there is no telling what could happen later.

The Detective tells her, "We'll have someone on watch, don't worry."

Later, when they are about to leave, Wilma says, "I wonder where the body must have come from. Was it from the city morgue or a butcher's freezer? If the body had been preserved and frozen for a while, then that much is called for, right?"

Detective Fellow is obviously curious but not precisely from her choice of words. "I'd like to know how come the body was moved here with no one knowing. What about your neighbors?"

Wilma does not hesitate when she answers. "They traveled for the holidays. Perhaps that's why I was targeted. Perhaps I was watched."

But she is uncertain whether that part is true.

"Don't worry about a thing, Miss Wade," Detective Fellow says. "We'll reach out to you when we hear something."

When they are gone, and she is once again left alone, Wilma checks the voicemail from the hospital. The voice she hears is sharp and pressured, like there are not enough words to be said:

We see the weather and understand how dangerous it would be for you to come here today. We send our best wishes to you and thank you for your consistent help. Happy holidays.

She does not reply to the message; instead, she calls her cousin.

Martha exclaims when she hears her voice. Then, she says, "How are you doing?"

In the background, Wilma can hear the laughter of little children. "I am fine. How are you?"

"The grandchildren keep me busy," she says.

Wilma does not tell her about the corpse or how uneasy it still makes her feel despite the body being moved. Instead, she laughs into the phone and says, "I am so glad you are all right."

The night is the longest she's ever experienced.

CHAPTER 4

Dr. McCall phones the Detective with more disturbing news. It is midafternoon, and Detective Fellow is halfway through files when he gets the call.

"The body was taken from the city morgue, Detective," the doctor says.

Fellow is perplexed, but now he knows that Miss Wade was right. Throughout the night, Fellow had thought about the entire situation, obsessing over the thought that perhaps the body being found was just a neatly spun web of conspiracy. With this new information, he was sure there was a secret plan laced between the lines, if that is possible?" he asks the doctor.

Dr. McCall has spent the entire morning wondering how removing a body from a place tight knitted with security might be possible but has come up short. "If someone has taken the body from the city morgue, then the person could be someone who's used to this place," he tells the Detective when he finds his voice in the haze.

"I don't understand," Fellow sounds upset; but that couldn't be helped either.

Dr. McCall speaks forwardly this time around. "We have had him in the freezer for weeks. It's highly impossible to take a body without one knowing since all the doors are always locked. Do you understand?"

"Then how come we have a case of a John Doe?" Fellow asks desperately.

Dr. McCall rubs a hand under his eyes. If the Detective is upset over this news, he will be furious when he hears the next one. But the doctor is careful in his choice of words. "We don't know how this was possible, but our forensics guys are trying to find something to put the culprit down."

The voice on the other end is chilled. "Let me know if you find anything."

This time, Dr. McCall does not hesitate. "I have another bad news, but I should let you know we are working on it now. I just wanted you to know for your information."

"What's that?" Fellow asks.

McCall says, "We have another person missing too. This time, it's a woman."

Fellow is undoubtedly tired but knows that shouting or getting agitated will not help matters. His voice is calm when he speaks. "Is it possible that both bodies were taken from the morgue at the same time?"

"That's what we believe, yes."

"And is there a relationship between the missing corpses?"

"We could not identify the bodies, but if there is a connection, we hope to find it soon."

When Detective Fellow hangs up the call, his first instinct is to call Miss Wade and tell her about the discovery, but that is not what he does. Sometimes he finds it weird how easily he hands out information about ongoing cases to her despite her being a civilian. The body was found in her house, but even Fellow knows she is only a victim.

Now, while Fellow is at the precinct not knowing what to do, Wilma is at her home, trying to write about the case. It isn't fiction as she is mainly accustomed to, but a version of the reality she has somehow found herself submerged in. She hates how it has gotten to her, but Wilma knows there is no turning back. She was ready to do anything if the culprit had used her house to play such a pitiful joke.

In her book, she writes a question and then underlines it, watching as her pen marks it repeatedly: Why would a criminal go through the trouble of placing a frozen body in front of my house?

She does not know the answer. But as her mind frames the question, she hears her phone ringing. Wilma sees the caller and notices that it is the Detective. She holds the phone away from her face for a second and wonders why she is being called again. Not that she is bothered about her position in this matter. Wilma does not want to feel it or believe it, but she is frightened about the response she'll get from Fellow.

She takes the call, finally. "Oh, hello, Detective," she says enthusiastically, hoping her voice does not betray her. "What have you found out?"

Fellow hesitates before he speaks. She can hear the tension in his voice. "I'm afraid you were right. The frozen corpse was from the city morgue. There is another missing corpse, but it's a woman this time."

Wilma can't believe what she's heard. She leans against the wall to keep herself from falling over from the shock. Without thinking, Wilma walks to her window and pushes the curtains aside. There are still traces of snow on the ground but not so much that she can't see the concrete. She needs to be sure there isn't another body outside for her.

She asks, "Did you identify either of them?"

She hears the crumpling of papers and sighs. He answers, "No, but Dr. McCall thinks the bodies may have been moved from the morgue around the same time. There is no definite proof, but they are searching for clues to help them track the culprit."

Wilma licks her lips and moves into the kitchen. Her hands are still wrapped around the phone, and as she presses it to her ears, she feels the coldness of it.

"What do you think must have happened?" she asks tentatively.

There are way too many scenarios in her head, but here, now, she is begging to be let into the mind of the Detective. He is a professional, she knows, so most of these things will make sense to him.

"We've been able to tell how they were both killed," he says instead and does not wait for her probing questions. "Both of them had gunshot wounds at the back of their heads. Quite dramatic, don't you think?

But Wilma has grown weary of the news, so she can't quite think yet. After the Detective has promised to call with more news, she goes quietly to her open book and scribbles quickly as if afraid she'll forget any word if she stops:

Who are the two victims? Why would anyone want to add her to the puzzle? Did the culprit make a mistake?

It's not long before the Detective calls again. Wilma thinks that perhaps he knows of her book and the questions and calls just at the right moment to divulge secrets and answers.

"We got the pictures of the missing bodies," he says to her without an introduction. "I will send the pictures over to your email address. See if you can identify any."

"Is that going to help?" she asks.

She imagines him nodding before speaking. "We need to know why you were targeted or if it was random. Try to look deeply, Miss Wade."

"Of course," her voice sounds pathetic with its high-pitched enthusiasm, but he does not comment on it. "Send them over."

"I'll stay on the line for a few minutes more," he says through clenched teeth. "If you recognize just one, please tell me."

Wilma knows the pictures have arrived in her mail when her phone beeps. She pauses, handheld out midway, afraid she'll hate the outcome of the end as much as the beginning. She can hear the Detective's ragged breathing and the crunching of leaves, knowing that he is walking and hoping for a burst of her voice in recognition of the photos.

Wilma wants to ask him what they'll think of her if she can't recognize the bodies; she wants to know if she'll become a suspect instead of a witness but can't find the right words to say. Her hesitation is alarming, mostly because she can't will herself to look.

"Are you still there?" he asks her.

She takes a deep breath and clicks on the photos. The man and the woman's photographs have been put side by side and locked behind her screen; she finds that the man differs from how she remembers him. When she'd found him underneath the snow, his skin looked rough and purple with markings against his body. Now, she sees he is white and pale but greatly human.

"Is this before he went missing?" she asks.

Fellow replies, "Yes... yes, what do you think?"

That's when she sees the uncanny resemblance. The woman's face also lights up the screen, and when Wilma stares fully into the tight skin of her face, Wilma almost drops her phone.

"Miss Wade?" he calls quietly. "Do you recognize any?"

Wilma is anything but weak, but, at this moment, she is reminded of her age. She's seen a lot of things in her lifetime, of course, but this one is too sudden that it startles her. A minute later, Wilma has composed herself considerably.

"Yes, I do," she replies. "This is Mr. Edward Worthington, and she is Mrs. Elizabeth Worthington. They don't live in the States, so I don't know why they'd be here."

Detective Fellow breathes a sigh of relief when he hears that. Now he is confident they have something they can work on. "And what's your relationship with them?"

She says, "I am friends with Edward's Aunt, Mrs. Maisie Worthington."

"Do you know if there ever were issues with the family? Do you know of anyone who would want to kill him?"

Wilma does not think she's the best fit to answer the questions since it has been a while since she spoke with Maisie, her nephew, and his wife. She barely considers herself a family friend anymore, considering how long it has been since she's seen them. Perhaps, she reckons, she couldn't quite recognize him at first.

"Maisie and her husband are estranged. Her brother passed away suddenly last year, from what I heard. His son would have inherited his estate. I hear it's worth millions. Do you think there's anything there?"

Detective Fellow stops in his tracks. Yes, he means to say, but his lips catch something else. "We can't be sure, but I'll have people check for connections. We won't leave any stone unturned, that's for sure."

Two heavily quiet days later, Wilma sees the Detective's car out front. He is wearing a leather jacket and baggy jeans like he's come straight out of an 80s movie. As Wilma opens the door and invites him in, she lets her mind wander around the thought of what he means with his fashion sense today.

In her living room, he makes no intention of sitting. She offers him tea. He respectfully declines. It's the first time he's refused tea. That's how she knows there is something he means to say.

"We've just discovered something interesting," he says to her.

"What?" That's what her eyes say.

"Mr. Edward was the heir to the fortune and the estate, and he disappeared one day. His wife, Elizabeth, would become the heir, with him turning up dead. That was the Will."

Wilma holds her left wrist with her right hand and sighs. She suddenly does not need the Detective to spill the words out. "Let me guess. The wife also disappeared, and since they are both dead, Maisie will become the heir."

"Clever, huh?" Fellow dusts the invisible creases off his jacket and looks up at her. "Can you see the web now? It's untangling before us."

"But she couldn't be able to do that, right?" Wilma imagines herself holding a gun and killing anyone her age. Granted, Maisie is not as old as she is. Even so, it seems far-fetched.

"That's what's interesting," he says to her. His voice is nothing more than a whisper now. "You told me she was estranged from her husband, but she isn't. She planned with him to murder the couple. How's that?"

CHAPTER 5

Wilma knows of the situation between her friend, Maisie, and her husband. She knows about how Maisie had asked him to leave. And he had. And she has since stopped talking with him. When Wilma tries to think about it, she realizes that what the Detective is saying will not be possible unless Maisie has been lying all along about being away from her husband. She tells the Detective this and stills herself for his response. She wants to believe Maisie and how impossible it would be for the woman to murder her family to inherit the family estate.

"We found evidence suggesting they still talk," Fellow tells her. "Some messages had been deleted, but we have the best agents. They have been able to bring those messages back. They are proof of conspiracy between Mrs. Maisie and her husband to murder the sole heirs of the estate."

"But they live in a villa on the Isle of White in the United Kingdom," Wilma tells him like she is teaching him about the geography of things. She is a retired teacher, of course, but there are still so many things she can't change. "How come the bodies were found in the States? Why would they go through the trouble of bringing the bodies here?"

"I don't think they brought the bodies here," Fellow tells her. "We think the couple came here on vacation weeks ago, and Maisie knew of this. From the messages, you could tell that she told her husband of this, and he came down to do the job."

Wilma's mind works around everything, trying to process the almost perfect conspiracy. She's always considered Maisie a friend. But if Maisie had pushed her under the bus, then perhaps there isn't any friendship there at all. It makes her sick to the bones. She wants nothing more than to take the first flight out to meet Maisie at her home and confront her for all the deaths, lies, and treachery, but despite all of the ache in her bones, she is not impulsive.

"I don't think she did all this without prior plans," Wilma says. Finally, her thoughts are coming together to form something coherent. Through the days when she heard nothing from Detective Fellow, she's been playing with these thoughts. She hasn't written them down on her note or tried to write them into a story she'll read next year at the hospital. She's thought of the culprit and how ridiculously cheap their tricks are. Did they think she was senile?

Now, she's seeing, for the first time, a twist she didn't think was possible. As much as she wants to argue with Fellow, she also knows it is meaningless. She's been tricked into believing a friendship of many years could mean something in the face of greed. This case and the entire situation taught her something about friendships that she will hold close for years to come.

"It's a carefully plotted murder," Fellow agrees with her.

"If I had to guess, I think Maisie remained in the U.K., so things don't look suspicious while her husband traveled down here to make the killings," she says. She is projecting her thoughts here now, but since he isn't disputing it, she continues, "But she must have known the suspicions would fall back on the family."

Detective Fellow raises one hand to scratch his beard. Wilma notices the overnight stubble and turns away. He says, "The messages are alarming."

"What?"

"The messages?" he lays the papers where he's printed the messages on the small table close to her favorite couch. "Here, look at these last messages she sent him."

"Oh, I haven't got my glasses," she says and walks away from him. He waits for her because he knows how invaluable her thoughts her in such cases. He has asked her before how interested she often is in such cases.

"I used to watch a lot of crime shows when I was much younger," she recalls. "Plus, I wanted to be a crime writer or a detective."

"A crime writer you are!"

"Oh, I wouldn't call myself that."

Wilma comes back now with her glasses and takes the papers. Fellow uses the tip of a pen to point out the last messages he needs her to see. That's what she sees before she gasps and looks up at him.

He reads the expression in her eyes. "That's right, Miss Wade. She's trying to reach him, but he seems to hide out."

"It sounds like she is desperate," Wilma adds, trying to think of a more plausible explanation. "Or wait! What if she had an original plan from that of her husband? What if, right now, she's searching for him because she knows the police will soon be on her?"

"He must have realized her plan right after taking the body here and fled," she says. "Have you found the body of the wife? He wouldn't have had the time to drop it if he realized the plans and then fled as well."

"We found the body," he says.

That's the thing about Wilma. She's always quick to deduce issues about twisted murder plots. He likes it when he brings out facts for her to open up and give her invaluable insight. That's why he is here.

"You found Elizabeth Worthington?" she asks. Her face tells him she thinks she has not heard well like there is an apology she wants to spill out in front of him for not being able to listen to his words.

"Yes," says Fellow. "The owner of a motel called this morning. She's been perceiving something terrible, and when she went to check, she found a body. The room was hot, so the body must have melted."

"He left in a hurry then," Wilma says. "If forensics check the room, perhaps they'd find proof he was there. Everything has to be based on evidence, right?"

He nods.

Wilma says, "I don't think we should let Maisie think she's become a suspect. She'll come over if she only thinks she will be questioned as a witness."

He agrees. "You should call her then."

Wilma dials her number and waits until the fourth ring before Maisie's voice comes through.

"Wilma?" She sounds unsure. "Is that you, dear?"

Wilma wants to cry from the memories she still has about Maisie, but she can't crumble into the phone. She says, "I'm afraid I don't have pleasant news, Maisie."

"What happened? Are you all right?"

Wilma tells her about the bodies and listens as Maisie gasps and sobs. When she tells her about the questioning, Maisie stops crying.

"I just thought they went for their usual holiday," she says. "I don't mind coming down for the questioning, but what can I say?"

"Detective Fellow will only need to ask you a few questions to clarify something," Wilma tells her.

"All right," she blows her nose. "I don't think I could sleep tonight. I have insomnia, but I think this could be worse."

After Wilma hangs up, she shuts her eyes and closes her heart to the good old memories.

CHAPTER 6

Wilma is the first person Maisie Worthington sees at the arrival concourse of the Barwick Airport. When their eyes meet, Maisie raises a hand over her head but does not move from where she's standing. It's Wilma who makes a move to her.

"Oh, hi, Maisie," Wilma says as she circles the woman in a firm embrace. "It's good you could come here on such short notice."

Maisie sniffs. And when Wilma loosens her hold on her body, she takes out a handkerchief to dab at her eyes. Wilma can't tell if she is crying or if this is just a practiced lie, but she trails a hand over Maisie's jacket, pity in her eyes.

"It's so terrible," Maisie confesses and looks past Wilma's shoulders at the throngs of people piling around. When her eyes finally meet Wilma's again, she sees that the older woman has got nothing but worry in her eyes. "I can't bear to think they've been dead for weeks. I worry for you too."

In her car, Wilma wants to ask why underneath Maisie's worried façade, there's still a missing piece. There is a puzzle that can instantly rip out all the perfectly placed lies she thinks Maisie and her husband have said to both her and the Detective. Still, Wilma knows that Maisie will understand the suspicions by saying that. Frankly, Wilma wants to give her the element of surprise to watch her expression, and she can't do that in this car. As much as she wants to believe this woman about her innocence, Wilma's heart will not let her. There are just too many holes in the story that need filling up.

"I understand the Detective wants to question me at your house," Maisie says as she shifts her weight in the car.

She is wearing expensive cologne and has got her hair braided. In the car, she wears lipstick, and when she catches Wilma staring, she says, "My lips feel dry. I hate it when they crack, you know."

The car smells of Jasmine and roses; even though Wilma is overly conservative about such things, she can tell they are expensive. To Wilma, it seems like Maisie is trying too hard to cover up the smell of guilt over her skin, but even Wilma can't be sure.

"Yes," she agrees. "The detective will ask you a few questions at my place."

Maisie nods and drops her hands to her thighs. Gently, she caresses the finger where her wedding band used to be. Now, there is just a space that screams in the car. Still, when Wilma glances down at her finger, she sees the line feverishly bright, like a scar, on the ring finger. It is almost like Maisie has had her ring until recently, tossing it away when she got the call. Didn't that tie her into everything?

Wilma thinks to herself as she drives, mapping out the most probable scenario: Perhaps this woman wanted to inherit the estate for herself but did not want to rope herself in. So she calls her estranged husband, who still loves her, into the game. He thinks they are doing it so they can run away together. Perhaps he misses her still, which is why he agreed. But she is hoping for Wilma to put two and two together and arrest him, removing all the blame from her.

But Wilma's scenario stops making sense when she considers the possibility of the police finding the husband, Mr. Samson Worthington, and then listening as he confesses and pulls her in. They already have some deleted conversations between her and her husband, which would tie them together. But if her scenario becomes real, Wilma is sure the police cannot find the husband.

She gives Maisie another sweeping glance and continues the drive back to her place. They do not speak to each other for the rest of the drive. While Wilma consciously tries to understand the gravity of the situation, Maisie is scrolling through her phone.

At her place, Wilma hurries into the kitchen to put the kettle on the stove. Maisie meets her there in the kitchen, and Wilma sees her clearly now with her makeup. Maisie does not look like a grief-stricken woman. But then again, Wilma can't classify anyone's level of grief. Perhaps Maisie is, in fact grieving in the only way she can. That is a possibility too.

"Your place is small," she observes, glancing around the small kitchen. Although the place is neat and has nothing that doesn't fit in, Wilma notices the disdain in those eyes. "Do you even like it here?"

Of course, she and Maisie have never been close friends. But once upon a time, Wilma had considered the idea of such a tight-knit friendship. Now that she looks back to that moment, she feels she has been limiting herself to the possibility of a closer friendship with a shallow woman like Maisie. She hates the feeling more than she hates the person, which is a good thing, at least to Wilma.

Wilma serves the tea in two cups and sips hers slowly since it is too hot. Maisie makes no move to take hers. She seems like she is thinking. "Why would anyone want to drop the bodies at your place?"

Wilma shrugs. Why didn't they wait for the Detective? "Let's wait until Detective Jason Fellow is here. He should be here any minute."

Maisie sighs and hugs her body closer.

When the Detective eventually arrives, Wilma offers him tea and sits with him in her living room. Maisie sits on a smaller chair opposite and crosses her feet like she has prepared for this moment for a long time. This scene suddenly reminds Wilma of her cousin and how, as she faced her cousin, she had felt powerful like a detective. That's how she feels now too.

"I just have a few questions for you, Mrs. Worthington," Detective Jason Fellow says, leaning forward. "Can you tell us where your estranged husband might be?"

She frowns and shakes her head before her lips can form the words. "I wouldn't know that, Detective. We have been estranged for years."

"Okay, but when did you speak to him last?" Fellow asks her.

She looks at Wilma as her frown deepens. "Am I here as a suspect or as a witness?"

"Just answer the questions, Maisie," Wilma tells her.

Maisie drags her feet on the floor and licks her lips. Wilma thinks she will explode soon, but she does not make a move to stop her. Perhaps it will be this moment that will throw her off course in the questioning.

Fellow repeats the question. "When was the last time you spoke with your husband, Mrs. Worthington?"

"We haven't spoken in years," she says flatly.

Wilma sighs. She was hoping Maisie would have a good enough explanation for what they have discovered. But with this blatant lie, Wilma is uncertain they can do anything about it. If Maisie is lying, perhaps, there is a truth hidden in every scene she's mapped out in her head.

Detective Fellow passes a paper across to her. "Can you tell us what you think that means?"

She takes it with both hands and leans back against the chair to skim through the paper. Wilma watches her and sees that her expression has changed. She is no longer composed. She looks frightened for whatever reason. Wilma notices a slight tremor in her hands.

Maisie stands up on her feet. "I don't know where you got these messages, but I am uncomfortable with them. I will contact my lawyer and…."

Fellow does not stand up, but Wilma thinks he is floating when he speaks. His voice contains a power she hasn't heard before. She can feel his controlled anger vibrating in the house.

He says, "We found your husband, Mrs. Worthington. I am certain you didn't think he'd be found, but you couldn't hide him away for long."

Wilma is surprised. This is a recent development she hasn't heard of before.

It is Maisie who shakes her head nervously. "You are bluffing."

But somehow, she knows he isn't.

"We had our men track down these deleted messages and where he was last seen. From there, tracking him to his current location and bringing him down here was relatively easy, which should tell you that you did a rather sloppy job keeping him hidden. He has given us a rather shocking confession," Fellow tells her.

But Wilma still does not understand the entire situation. If Maisie and her husband murdered the couple to inherit the estate, they could have let the body continue to be at the morgue. What was the need to bring the body to the front of her house?

Maisie cries. Not the kind she did at the airport to elicit pity, but a crying out of frustration and thwarted plans. Before long, Wilma hears the sounds of sirens outside her house.

"You are under arrest for the murder of Mr. Edward and Mrs. Elizabeth Worthington," Fellow tells her.

Sheriff Riley comes into the house and takes her away. When Wilma is alone with Detective Fellow, she asks him the questions she can't find the answers to.

"Why did they place the body in front of my house if they were simply trying to run away after inheriting the estate?" she asks.

Fellow says, "At first, they wanted to blame you. Mr. Samson had not been banking on you being back returning holidays with your cousin."

"And he wanted the police to think I ran away to meet my cousin after killing and hiding the body in the snow?"

"The bodies were at the morgue, of course, but perhaps they felt, further along, we'd discover. They needed to put someone under the bus; you were the only person they could think of."

Wilma sighs and runs a hand through her hair. "They didn't deserve to be murdered because of a stupid inheritance."

"I know," Fellow says.

Alone, Wilma goes into her room, climbs into bed, and closes her eyes. She is tired and cold and wants to sleep, but after a while, she knows it is impossible. So, Wilma calls her cousin, who takes it almost immediately.

Wilma says, "Well, cousin, you wouldn't believe what happened!"

The End

INJURED ON NEW YEAR'S

A JANE AND KENNEDY DANIELS
MYSTERY

CHAPTER 1

Jane Daniels had always been a bit of a sleuth. She loved mysteries, crime novels, and drama. One of her favourite pastimes was to curl up on the sofa with her wife, Kennedy, watching serial killer documentaries and trying to piece everything together before the celebrity narrator revealed who the killer was. The fact that Kennedy enjoyed the same thing was one thing that first attracted Jane to her wife. They both loved mysteries, and Jane had a talent for solving crimes. Jane looked at mysteries as though they were puzzles. She saw them as just missing that vital piece, and she needed to be the one to find it.

Jane also loved a good bargain. She loved hunting around shops for that particular bargain item she could brag about. She considered every shopping expedition an excuse to hunt for treasure. The X on her mental treasure map was always the location of the most discounted item in whatever particular store she was in. Jane loved the after-Christmas and January sales the most. All the must-have items, new gadgets, and things she could put aside for the following year were at the best possible discount price, making them a definite, *Yes, please!* It was a yearly tradition to check out what treasures she could find.

Meanwhile, Kennedy was the cyber-wizard of the family. She loved it when Jane came home with a new gadget. She loved nothing more than adding to her electronics collection, especially anything she could use to make everyday life easier and more enjoyable. Kennedy had practically automated every inch of their home. It was like living in the future, and they loved it.

Kennedy was a reasonably intelligent woman. She was very proud of her MIT education. Her keen intellect was why Detective Inspector Arthur Gottfried often consulted her regarding some of his more complex cases. She had helped with many instances that year alone, and even more since she had moved to the UK full time from her home in Boston, Massachusetts.

Jane and Kennedy had a lot in common, making their marriage a joy to behold. Their friends always admired the love they had for each other. Their friends often referred to their successful marriage as #couplegoals.

Jane used to envy her family and friends for having the one thing she didn't – A child of her own. She loved being 'fun aunty Jane' but craved being called 'Mummy' the most. After their near miss on Halloween, Jane and Kennedy had decided it was finally time to start a family. However, Jane's run-in with the law on Boxing Day had momentarily put a hold on their plans. But as the New Year approached, it signalled a fresh start, the start of the next part of their journey in life together. Jane could hardly wait.

* ❄ ❄ ❄ *

Their unexpected trip to Italy had been fun and exactly what they needed after Jane was arrested on Boxing Day. Jane was glad that everything with Sam and the jewellery theft had been sorted and she could go back to life as usual.

It was time to pack up their things and return home to London. Unfortunately, since it was New Year's Day, travelling was sure to be a nightmare. The airports would be packed; Jane would have loved to stay a little longer, but a New Year's Day ticket was the only one available on such short notice. They couldn't stay for another two weeks – no matter how much Jane wanted to.

The mayor was hosting yet another ball; Jane and Kennedy had been humming and hawing over whether to attend. After the Halloween Horrors party, it would either go wonderfully, and they would be able to make new memories, or they would be forced to relive the painful ones from the judge's fatal shooting.

But Jane had never been one to turn down an invitation, and Kennedy followed wherever Jane went. So, they booked their ticket and waved goodbye to their spontaneous Italian getaway.

Jane rolled over in bed and snuggled up to Kennedy. She pushed a strand of her beautiful black ringlets out of her face and kissed her forehead. She was so lucky to have such a wonderful wife.

The hotel they were staying in was remarkably fancy. The architecture was beautiful and oozed history. While it was amazing, it was a far cry from their technologically advanced home. Jane looked to the tea and coffee facilities: a small kettle and a few packets of instant coffee, tea bags, and sugar with a small jug of milk tucked in the under-cabinet fridge. For such a short trip, it would do. Jane and Kennedy couldn't wait to get home to their coffee machine. It would have their favourite coffees freshly brewed waiting for them when they arrived – all thanks to a click of an app Kennedy had designed.

The mayor's New Year's Ball was rumoured to be just as lavish as the last. Celebrities, sports stars, and influential people were all invited. The paparazzi were even more excited about this ball after the fateful events of the Halloween party she hosted. They were hoping for an even better story this time.

"Kennedy," Jane sighed. "We must start packing to make it home in time for the mayor's ball."

Kennedy groaned and pulled a pillow over her head.

"Five more minutes…" a soft snoring sound could be heard, muffled by the pillow.

Jane chuckled and moved the pillow off Kennedy's head.

"Sorry, babe. We don't have time," she glanced at the clock. "It's already seven. The airport is going to be packed."

The pair rolled out of bed and rubbed the sleep from their eyes. Jane quickly headed to the kitchenette to brew fresh coffees. The strong aroma filled the room. There was no way that they would get to the airport on time without a potent pick-me-up.

"I do love the French brew coffee we have back home, but man, this Italian coffee tastes good," Kennedy hummed, taking a sip.

"We can pick some up at the airport, and then you can get one of your fancy new gadgets to add more to our shopping list when we get home," Jane smiled as she packed her suitcase.

Kennedy nodded with a smile; she had picked up a few new AI gadgets on their trip and was already planning how to use them.

"But if we are ever going to get home, you better start packing before we miss our flight and have to spend the next two weeks living at the airport waiting for a flight home," Jane joked.

Kennedy started throwing clothes into their suitcases randomly, hoping to get it done as quickly as possible. Jane worried that Kennedy seemed anxious.

"How are you feeling about the New Year's Ball tonight?" Jane looked at Kennedy intently. They hadn't had much time to talk about it.

"I don't know, honestly. I don't think it could be any worse than the Halloween party," she chuckled.

"You're right about that," Jane cracked a huge grin, glad to see that Kennedy was in good spirits. "Arthur said he wants to meet us at the airport around eight sharp."

"Okay," Kennedy started. "Just a few more moments alone," Kennedy slinked across the room, wrapping her arms around her wife's waist, hugging her from behind, resting her chin on Jane's shoulder.

"Our mornings together have been so short lately. And soon, I will have to share you with a little one. Until then, I want to soak up as much time alone with you as possible," Kennedy kissed Jane's cheek softly.

"We haven't even started looking at options yet," Jane laughed.

"I know, but I can feel it's going to happen soon."

Jane looked at Kennedy just in time to catch a pout.

"Okay, five more minutes. Then we have to get out of here."

Jane and Kennedy lay on the bed, fully dressed and packed, and closed their eyes, enjoying each other's company for a moment longer. When Jane opened her eyes again, the clock said seven-thirty. They had laid down for longer than they had meant to, and had to get out of there, stat.

Grabbing their suitcases, they headed out of the room and down to the hotel lobby to check out.

* ❋ ❋ ❋ *

"There he is, Kennedy," Jane tugged on Kennedy's arm. Arthur was holding a tray of three coffees ahead of them. The airport was indeed packed. Everyone was trying to get home after their New Year's Eve celebrations.

"Here you are! I was worried you two would sleep in," Arthur handed the girls their coffees. Jane and Kennedy giggled.

"We almost did. Kennedy wouldn't wake up!" Jane winked.

After a little small talk, the group headed through the airport. They collected the tickets they purchased the night before online and headed to check in the luggage and stroll through customs.

The line was longer than they had expected. It was too bad that they hadn't had the foresight to book a return flight. Returning the stolen Medici jewellery was the only thing that they had considered when they decided to go to Italy in the first place.

They had a lot of fun in Italy. The museum they visited was incredible, making Jane and Kennedy want to learn more about Europe and European history.

"Can I have the window seat this time, guys?" Jane pleaded. She loved watching the buildings turn into blobs. And when the plane was high enough, you see the tops of the clouds underneath them.

"Yes, babe. Of course, you can," Kennedy said, wrapping her arms around Jane's shoulder and pulling her in tight. "Anything for you," she winked.

They had just enough time to grab some breakfast. It was a good thing, too, as Kennedy's stomach growled loudly. Wandering through the duty-free area, Jane picked up a few bags of dark roast coffee beans for Kennedy; Arthur was not engaging in the shopping experience, so he settled down with his book, waiting patiently. Kennedy stumbled upon a small pushcart selling fresh pastries. The smell of Canoli filled her nostrils, making her mouth water.

"Oh my god," Kennedy muttered. "I need to eat one, and I need to eat one right now."

Kennedy bought a few, sitting down to share them with the group while they waited to board their flight.

"I hope you know that you deserve the world, Kennedy," Jane smiled and stared into Kennedy's deep brown eyes.

"What makes you say that?"

"I love you so much. I cherish every day we spend together. I just wanted you to know how much I care for you." Jane wrapped her arm around Kennedy's shoulders and pulled her in for a quick kiss.

Arthur rolled his eyes at the public display of affection but smiled to himself behind his book. Suddenly, a loud beep sounded in the lounge, and a feminine Italian voice spoke shortly after the spokesperson reiterated the message in English and a few other languages.

"I guess it's time to board. Let's get this show on the road!" Jane cheered, excited to be on her way back home.

Lost in translation, none of the group realised their seats were separated. Jane had been looking forward to the window seat only to find that she and Kennedy had booked aisle seats, separated by a stranger. And Arthur was sitting right at the back of the plane. But at least they were heading home. Kennedy and Jane convinced the man in the middle seat to swap places so that they could sit next to each other. They had a smooth but exhausting flight home.

CHAPTER 2

"Where did you put our clothes for tonight?" Kennedy asked Jane. The ball was starting in a few hours, and they needed to get ready.

"In the wardrobe. I'll go get everything," Jane smiled. She loved doing small things for Kennedy. She worked so hard, whether working with her programming clients or sleuthing. She deserved to be taken care of sometimes.

Jane was a stay-at-home wife. She had given up her career after they married with plans of starting a family. But life had other plans, and their dream to start a family had been put on hold, for reasons neither could remember. Perhaps that's why Jane shopped as much as she did – to fill the hole in her heart and the time she thought she would have been caring for a little one. As such, Jane also spent a lot of time baking and reading. She loved to sleuth, too, and their favourite pastime was watching mystery series on TV.

Jane brought their outfits out of their bedroom into the living room. Jane opened her garment bag first and removed a beautiful floor-length dress. With a sweetheart neckline, the dress shone with silver and sparkles all over.

"Wow. I'm speechless," Kennedy said. "That dress is going to look amazing on you."

Jane blushed and pulled out Kennedy's outfit. First, was a navy-blue dress that would hit the mid-thigh area and hug her body. The second piece of the outfit was a silver sequinned blazer.

"Wow, that is... interesting. Are you sure I should wear that?" Kennedy asked.

Jane's face fell, she knew it wasn't ideal, but she tried her best to find something Kennedy would feel comfortable in.

"I was hoping we could wear matching outfits. See?" Jane pointed to the dress and the blazer, which reflected the light in every direction. "And they're festive. Everyone knows you wear sparkles on New Year's." Kennedy smiled at Jane. Her happiness was infectious.

"The blazer isn't the issue, babe," she shook her head. "Why the dress?"

"Oh, that. Well, I bought them last minute. And online. My options were pretty limited. It was either this or a cheetah print mini dress. I thought this was the safer option."

Kennedy burst out laughing at the idea of her wearing a cheetah print mini dress. She would indeed be the talk of the party.

"Okay, let's get dressed then. We'll meet Arthur there!"

* ❋ ❀ ❋ *

When Jane and Kennedy arrived at the New Year's Ball, they weren't surprised that the mayor had pulled out all the stops. It seemed to be the mayor's thing, putting on an extravagant ball.

The walkway to the double doors was lined with gold carpeting instead of red this time, and the attendees were unmasked. No costumes. Everyone could see who was there.

The paparazzi were having a field day. So many celebrities, sports stars, and influential figures were mingling and chatting. Some of them even did the paparazzi a kindness and posed for photos. The mayor spared no expense and hired someone to do her own version of a "glam cam" that took videos of celebrities in slow motion.

"Hello, Mrs and Mrs Daniels," a voice whispered behind them.

Kennedy whipped her head around. After the last party, she wasn't taking any chances and had her senses on high alert.

"Just me!" Arthur winked.

"Not funny, Arthur," Kennedy frowned, poking him on the arm.

Arthur was a great friend and a fantastic detective, but sometimes he could be slightly daft. Kennedy had almost been murdered at the last ball held on the premises, so it wasn't the best place to poke some fun.

"Sorry, sorry," he paused. "Also, I'm sorry I missed you at the airport after we landed, it was so crowded, and I needed to get home to get ready."

"No worries, Arthur; how was your flight?" Kennedy asked.

Kennedy wasn't actually expecting a response. Arthur wasn't usually the type to talk about monotonous details. He typically had a purpose behind his words.

"Fun, actually," Arthur replied with a mischievous grin.

The girls exchanged a look, grinning. What had happened?

"Care to elaborate?" Jane asked.

Kennedy and Jane waited expectantly. Even though celebrities surrounded them, Arthur had clearly met someone very important. Jane and Kennedy had very different types of people they looked up to. Jane admired many women on the cooking channel, and Kennedy fancied people who were super intelligent and worked with AI and other technology. Arthur blushed before responding.

"My ex-flatmate, Mary, was on the plane. She was in the seat right next to me, spent her Christmas visiting her son. It was a blast from the past. I think I may have told you about her before," Arthur looked between Jane and Kennedy, who looked back blankly.

"Apparently not. Anyway, she was my flatmate after I graduated from university, she is a nurse now. Her skills proved very handy after a few rough nights out...." Arthur trailed off, seeing the grins on Kennedy and Jane's faces.

They had never seen Arthur so excited. Looking back, they couldn't remember him showing much interest in any woman or having a relationship while they had known him.

"I'm sorry, I'm rambling; let's go inside," Arthur blushed.

Jane, Kennedy, and Arthur walked up the steps and entered the grand building. Sparkly decorations hung from every wall, and a giant disco ball hung from the ceiling. It reflected light in every direction as it spun. It was stunning, awe-inspiring.

The tables below had beautiful crystal centrepieces, and there were flecks of glitter all over the place; even the silverware was sparkling. Somehow, the whole building smelled of sweet champagne. It was intoxicating.

"Wow, the mayor has outdone herself this time!" Jane smiled.

She started walking down the stairs, still admiring the beautiful decorations. The music could be heard more clearly, now, and an Ariana Grande song was playing. Jane turned her head around to ensure Kennedy was walking right behind her and suddenly felt her foot slip off the polished steps. She landed at the bottom of the stairs with a loud thud, and her world faded to black.

CHAPTER 3

Beep, beep, beep. Jane groaned. Was her alarm going off already? She didn't remember anything from the night before. She didn't even remember whether she had been drinking or not. Jane tried to stretch out her hand to reach for Kennedy, and a sharp pain shot through her arm.

She groaned even louder. *What's going on?*

Slowly opening her eyes, Jane was greeted by a bright fluorescent light. It stung a little, and she quickly closed them. *Am I dead? Is this the white light?*

"Jane, are you awake?" A shoulder touched her arm softly. Jane would know that touch anywhere. It was Kennedy. A smile crossed her face as she attempted to nod.

"Where am I?" Jane croaked.

"You are in hospital. You fell down the stairs at the mayor's ball," she said softly. "You're going to be okay, but you passed out. You have a broken leg. Do you remember anything?"

Jane closed her eyes, trying to remember but couldn't. Slowly, she shook her head, only to be left feeling dizzy by the motion. Jane tried opening her eyes again. She wanted to know more about what happened. She was clumsy, sure, but enough to break her leg falling down some stairs? Her vision started to clear, and she could make out the outline of Kennedy.

"Hi," she croaked, cracking a small smile, "I'm good."

Kennedy laughed and smiled, brushing Jane's tangled brown hair off her face.

"You had to have surgery to reset the bone you broke. Are you in pain?"

Jane shook her head gently. The IV in her arm was pumping enough painkillers to mask the pain from her leg.

"No, I am a little groggy, I ache a little, but nothing I can't handle. I am thirsty, though. Can I have some water?" Jane asked.

Without hesitation, Kennedy was up on her feet, grabbing Jane a cold glass of water. Helping Jane sit up, she gave her a drink before settling down next to her. It was quiet, apart from the rhythmic beeps of the machines in the room. Kennedy moved closer to the bed Jane was lying on and sat down softly. She grabbed Jane's hand and looked into her beautiful blue eyes.

"Gosh, I was so worried about you. The floor wasn't even that slippery," Kennedy chuckled. "My clumsy wife strikes again."

A nurse hurried into the room to check Jane's charts. She mumbled to herself and nodded before offering Kennedy a small, almost awkward smile.

"Thanks, Mary," Kennedy grinned as the nurse hurried to her next patient.

Jane smiled when something clicked. Kennedy had called the nurse Mary, and Arthur had recently run into his ex-flatmate, Mary, who was a nurse, on his return flight to London.

"Is my nurse Arthur's roommate?"

"Yes, she's not as fun as Arthur described, though. Strictly business," Kennedy chuckled.

Usually, Arthur had a pretty good read on people. If they knew each other well, it was strange that she would be that different from his description. But it had been a long time since they had last seen each other.

Suddenly, a commotion from the nurse's station just a little down the hall alerted Jane and Kennedy to a new arrival to the ward. Jane's face lit up; that fuss could only mean one person. The door flung open.

"Jane! Oh, just look at you! You poor thing," Jane's mum stood at the door with a gift basket.

She frowned and looked around the room. "Thank goodness you're okay. I came as soon as I heard what happened."

Jane grinned at her mum. They were so close when she was growing up, and she was one of her best friends. When Kennedy and Jane married, they grew apart a little, but their bond was still strong. Her mom walked over to her bedside cautiously.

"Hi Kennedy, it's so good to see you," she said, bending down to hug Kennedy, who briefly hugged her back.

Her mother was delighted with Jane's choice to marry Kennedy. Of all the women she could have chosen, Kennedy treated her like a queen in a way that no other woman could. She was compassionate and loving and, most importantly, made Jane happy. A parent couldn't ask for a better daughter-in-law.

"Do you mind giving us a moment?" she smiled sweetly.

"Sure, I'll go get some tea. Would you like one?" Kennedy asked.

"Please," Jane's mother replied with a sweet smile.

Jane looked up at her mother. They looked similar, other than her mother's dyed blonde hair. It suited her so well, but Jane had tried blonde once, and she definitely couldn't pull it off.

"How are you, really?" her mother asked, a look of worry and concern painting her face.

It was a mother's job to worry about her daughter. Jane's heart sank in her chest. She so desperately wanted a child that she could be concerned about. After breaking her leg, it became more apparent that a child was the missing piece in her life. Laying around all morning had offered her a lot of time to think about her life.

"I'll be okay. I'm just tired," Jane yawned.

She would love to go back to sleep. Her experience in the hospital had been relatively uneventful, but regardless, she was exhausted. The pain in her leg was bothering her, and being woken up by nurses at all hours of the night was disorienting. As she was about to open her mouth, her mum interrupted.

"Get some rest. I'll check in on you later. I don't want to get in the way of your recovery," she leaned down, kissed Jane on the forehead, and left the room.

"Leaving so soon?" Kennedy asked, surprised when she returned with the teas.

"Jane's going to get some rest."

"Oh well, in that case, I'll take you home," Kennedy smiled.

Kennedy wished Jane a good night, placing several soft kisses on her forehead and allowing her time to rest. Jane felt better knowing Kennedy was accompanying her mother home; she didn't like the idea of her mother travelling around London alone at that time of evening.

That night, Jane drifted in and out of sleep. She had a dream that there was shouting in the hospital and a huge commotion; it was a vivid dream. It had felt almost real. But by morning, it was hazy.

* ✳ ❇ ✳ *

The following day, Jane woke still feeling sleepy after a night of fitful sleep. It wasn't long before Mary came in to deliver her meds. Jane's stomach growled loudly. She couldn't remember the last time she had eaten and was famished.

Mary handed Jane her meds and checked her vitals. She worked silently, her face serious. Jane wanted to get to know Arthur's friend better but could tell she was strictly business, as Kennedy had described her.

An orderly arrived with a trolly carrying breakfast. A small pot of tea with a jug of milk and sugar, fresh orange juice, scrambled eggs, and a slice of whole meal toast. Jane was salivating at the thought of eating a hot meal, even if it was hospital quality.

"How are you feeling? Did you get a good night's rest?" asked the orderly.

"I had a strange dream," Jane started.

"That is expected after sedation and the painkillers you are on," Mary said plainly.

"It felt so real. I could swear I heard a couple arguing in the room next to me. I even felt like I woke up ready to yell for them to be quiet, but I'm not sure," Jane said, sipping her juice.

Mary and the orderly exchanged an awkward glance, and the orderly hurried out of the room, leaving Mary and Jane alone.

"It was just a dream. There is no one in the room next to you. It is closed for the next few days while it is sanitised," Mary stated.

Jane nodded and continued to eat her breakfast. The more the sedation wore off, the clearer her mind became. She concentrated, trying to piece together what was real and what was not. Hospitals were usually quiet places except for emergencies, but she was sure now that it wasn't a dream.

"It wasn't a dream. I remember. I heard arguing," Jane said, a little panicked.

Mary's face stayed expressionless.

"Your vitals are fine. I shall leave you to rest," Mary said, beginning to leave. Mary stopped at the door turning back to look Jane in the eye, "I assure you, Mrs Daniels, no one is using that room for a few more days. Delusion after sedation is perfectly normal, do not stress about it."

And with that, Mary left Jane alone.

. ✳ ❋ ✳ .

When Kennedy arrived later that morning, Jane was eager to discuss what she had heard. The more she thought about it, the more she knew in her heart it was not a dream, and she wanted someone to listen to her.

"I know Mary said no one was in that room, but Kennedy, I know what I heard. Yes, I may have confused it as a dream before. But my mind is clear. I heard a man and a woman arguing," Jane insisted.

Kennedy sat on the edge of Jane's bed, taking her hand and stroking it gently.

"Okay, baby, I believe you. No need to get overly excited. Mary finished her shift shortly before your mother and I left, and we saw her leaving. She wouldn't be aware of anything that happened next door," Kennedy assured her.

Jane took in Kennedy's words and nodded along. Then, a thought occurred to her; butterflies rushed in her stomach at the thought.

"What we need to do is get a look in that room," Jane chirped, attempting to get out of bed.

"Oh sweetie, calm down," Kennedy chuckled, helping Jane back into bed. "Ever the budding detective."

"Kennedy...."

"Jane, what you heard was probably a doctor and nurse arguing about a patient. You are in a hospital. After all, it can happen. Or even two worried parents taking their anxiety out on each other. Nothing to worry about."

CHAPTER 4

When Kennedy got home that night, she couldn't get her conversation with Jane out of her head. Jane had been so insistent about what she had heard. She might not have heard the words of the exchange, but Jane knew something was amiss. Kennedy couldn't put her figure on it but knew she couldn't leave it to rest. Picking up her phone, she dialled Arthur's number.

"Evening Kennedy, how can I help you?" Arthur asked.

"Hi Arthur, can you come round? I want to discuss something with you."

"I'm on my way," Arthur said, ending the call.

Fifteen minutes later, Arthur arrived. Kennedy had a pot of tea and a store-bought Victoria sponge ready and waiting. The cake wasn't nearly as nice as anything Jane could make, but it would do the job for this conversation. Kennedy reiterated what Jane had insisted on to Arthur, who listened intently.

"You know, Kennedy, without it being called in, we can't venture into the hospital room. We have no authority there."

"I know, but maybe if we got a look into the room, it might help us, even if it is nothing. It would at least ease Jane's mind and let her get some rest," Kennedy insisted.

Arthur checked his watch. Mary would still be on shift. He could venture to the hospital and pretend to be checking in on Jane, and perhaps Mary would allow him a peek inside. Arthur agreed to look into it further and headed to the hospital.

. * ✳ * .

The next day, Jane woke with an unsettling feeling in her stomach. She hadn't been able to get the arguing out of her head, and it frustrated her that she was powerless even to take a peek. What if something had happened and someone lay dead in the next room? What if she was overthinking things out of boredom? Jane felt like she was going crazy.

"So, Jane, how are you doing? Sorry I couldn't get here sooner," Arthur smiled, bringing in a small bouquet of flowers for her bedside table.

"These are beautiful, thank you, Arthur; I'm doing better than I was the other day," Jane smiled.

Arthur sat beside the bed and waited for Kennedy to join him. When the door was closed, Jane's eyes bounced between them. Her skin itched as it did when she was about to be dragged into another case. Excitement pooled in her stomach.

"What's going on?" she asked.

"Kennedy told me what you heard the other night. She was adamant that you wouldn't settle until we looked into it further. But of course, we couldn't do that without cause," Arthur began.

Jane's pulse raced as her eyes danced between Kennedy and Arthur. Kennedy looked exhausted, like she hadn't slept at all. And on closer inspection, so did Arthur.

"I came by last night on the pretence that I was stopping by for a visit. I ventured into the wrong room by mistake. It was then that Mary found me, and I informed her of my findings. She called it in so I could be here on official police business," Arthur said.

"So, what did you find?" Jane asked, sitting up a little taller.

"The room was previously used by a man named Albert Gladstone, or at least that's what the records show. When I did some digging, we could find nothing on the man. Except the name was very similar to an alias used by a man once a bodyguard for a billionaire," Kennedy said.

"Yes, so we looked into his employer and found he had been reported missing three days ago," Arthur finished.

Jane waited patiently for them to continue. They were being vague, perhaps worried about protocol, but if something had happened, technically speaking, she was a witness.

"Have you ever heard of Mr Albert Candlestone?" Arthur asked.

Jane nodded. Of course, she had heard Albert Candlestone; who hadn't? He was one of the wealthiest men alive and had created a vast empire in the robotics industry. Kennedy looked up to him and thought he was a true innovator who deserved a good reputation and financial success. Kennedy had hoped to meet him one day.

"He's the billionaire that's gone missing. We're trying to track him down. Kennedy and I were up all-night hacking into systems, trying to figure out if any of his devices have pinged, but everything is so well encrypted that we haven't made much progress," he paused, and his face scrunched. "Any progress, really."

Jane knew how skilled Kennedy was at this sort of thing. She had managed to hack into systems previously thought unhackable. So, if she struggled with this, Jane knew how frustrated Kennedy would be. With the missing man being a personal hero of Kennedy's, Jane worried for her wife all the more.

Jane looked over at Kennedy. She looked exhausted, with bags under her eyes. All-nighters are expected when investigating cases, but Jane typically was around to make breakfast, encourage Kennedy to take naps, and care for her. This time, she had been alone. Guilt stabbed Jane. If only she had been looking where she was going, but then again, if she hadn't been in that hospital room, they wouldn't be looking into a missing billionaire—everything happens for a reason.

"Any theories as to what happened?" Jane asked.

Arthur shook his head. "None."

Though sad for Kennedy and Arthur that their all-nighter didn't amount to any leads, Jane got excited. This was her time to shine. She lived to find the missing piece of the puzzle. It was just the pick-me-up she needed. She loved sleuthing, and though she hadn't talked to Arthur yet, she had decided to get her licence to be a private investigator in the New Year. She had thought about it for a while, wanting to give her life more purpose than simply shopping and baking. It had been the plan before she had discussed starting a family, and her plan hadn't changed.

Kennedy and Jane were relatively well off but not rich. Comfortable. Having a child would make money tighter, so they would have a bigger safety net if Jane could work and put some money aside. That was the argument she had prepared for Kennedy should the need arise.

"I'll fill you in on what we have so far," Kennedy told Jane all the case details.

Mr Candlestone was in London on a business trip. A new technological advancement in biotic limbs for wounded soldiers. An advancement that was making waves for good reasons and bad. It would be life-changing for those who benefited, but other companies were working on similar things. Albert Candlestone had simply got there first, putting others' lifelong work on the scrap heap.

No one had seen him for days. He was considered to be a missing person at that point. When a comprehensive search with his tech team back had turned up empty, that's when they tried his devices, but even his wearable tech watch had turned up empty. It was as if the man had vanished.

They'd also searched databases for arrests, hospital records, and parking tickets with no luck.

"Have you checked the hospital databases? I mean, I'm in a hospital. If you were trying to find me, my name would appear in the system, right? You said the room next to me was used with the alias of one of his ex-employees. Why not search under former and current employee names and their aliases?"

"That's a lot of names Jane," Kennedy offered gently, she knew Jane wanted to help, but Kennedy was too exhausted to do an intense search.

"Wait, I remember reading an article about him once. He

commented that he once booked a hotel under his ex-wife's name to avoid the paparazzi. Try searching her name too," Jane chirped.

"I remember that article, good catch," Kennedy grinned.

Arthur nodded, taking his notepad from his coat pocket and jotting down his notes as he left the room.

CHAPTER 5

Arthur walked down the hall, still fervently looking at his notepad and writing. As he was about to write the last line of his thoughts, he bumped into someone.

"I'm so sorry about that," he looked up and was surprised to see yet another old friend.

"Daniella Fitzpatrick? Is that you?"

The woman nodded and smiled.

"It's Dr Fitzpatrick, now. But, you can still call me Dannie."

Arthur smiled in return. How bizarre that he had run into Dannie, too, his ex-girlfriend, from when he was in university. What were the chances of bumping into Mary on the plane and now Dannie in the hospital? For a second, Arthur thought divine forces were trying to send him a message.

"So, you ended up getting into medical school? I told you all that worrying over the UCAT was for nothing! I bet you killed it," Arthur grinned.

"Interesting choice of words Mr Detective Inspector," Dannie laughed.

They had parted amicably, and there were no hard feelings. Arthur had wanted to pursue his passion. And Dannie had wanted to pursue her dream of becoming a doctor. Now that they had both achieved their dreams, Arthur knew that they had made the right decision to split up. Too many things could have gone wrong if they had tried to stay together. Who knew they would end up meeting again like this? Perhaps it was a sign.

Dannie extended her arms out for a hug and pulled him in tightly.

"It's so good to see you, Arthur. Why are you in the hospital? Everything okay?" she looked concerned.

Of course, she would assume he was in the hospital due to an injury. He looked exhausted from the all-nighter sleuthing with Kennedy. Arthur told Dannie about Jane's tumble down the stairs at the New Year's Ball, and Dannie offered her sympathy.

"Why don't we meet for coffee later? I have to do some things for work, which is relatively time-sensitive."

"Of course, Arthur," Dannie nodded. "Come find me later in my office in the basement. Room 189, right next to the morgue. You can't miss it."

Arthur bid Dannie a farewell and continued walking down the hall. Things kept getting stranger for him. Something was off, but Arthur put it down to the nostalgia from meeting old friends as his memories flooded back to happier times.

Kennedy had brought a pack of playing cards with her to try and give Jane something else to focus her mind on. But no matter how many times Jane won at Go Fish or Snap, she insisted on prying for as much information as possible about Mr Candlestone. She wanted to know where he was last seen, with whom he was last seen, and any other clue that could help find him.

"Jane, please," Kennedy sighed. "I've told you everything I know. Let's take some time and sit here, the two of us, and enjoy each other's company. I feel this case is bigger than just a missing person case."

Jane tugged at Kennedy's arm and scooted over in the small bed, making room for her wife to lay down. Kennedy got into the bed and snuggled up against Jane. There was no place she would rather be. Jane had missed feeling Kennedy beside her and absentmindedly stroked Kennedy's hair, entwining her fingers in Kennedy's curls.

"I want to talk about something," Jane whispered.

"What about?" Kennedy yawned.

"When I talked to my mum yesterday, I realised just how badly I want to have a child with you," a tear dripped down her face.

Kennedy looked up at Jane, wiping away her tears and pulling her close for a tight embrace.

"We tried a donor before, and it didn't work, perhaps looking into IVF might be an option. I know it would be pricey, but you can't put a price on a child. And we could even use the same donor," Jane continued.

"He was a good donor. Great family history, a long line of highly educated relatives. Tall, dark, handsome, and those blue eyes. I still remember them," Kennedy grinned, her own excitement growing at the idea.

"When can we start?" Jane asked.

"Let's get you discharged from here first. We can start looking into IVF as soon as possible. But it's still going to take time, and I need you at full health," Kennedy grinned, giving Jane a gentle kiss.

The two lay in silence for a few minutes, simply wrapped in each other's arms. Jane imagined her life with a child. An image flashed in her mind, a little boy with ringlets like Kennedy and a little girl with blue eyes like herself. She wasn't fussed if it was a girl or boy, as long as it was happy and healthy. She would paint the nursery grey, neutral enough to work with a boy or a girl, maybe do some yellow accents. They would have to move Kennedy's office space out of the second bedroom, though, and she had no idea where all her equipment would go.

Kennedy was thinking about how Jane would make such a wonderful mum. She was compassionate, caring, and nurturing – a born mother. There was nobody she'd ever consider having a child with except for her. Kennedy imagined building new gadgets with her son, flying a drone with a daughter, and raising her to be intelligent and strong like her.

"As soon as possible," Kennedy hummed, smiling to herself.

"Okay," Jane exhaled deeply, content with her daydreams. "I love you."

"I love you more," Kennedy sighed contentedly.

* ✳ ❋ ✳ *

Jane and Kennedy fell into a deep, peaceful sleep. Jane was still recovering from surgery, and Kennedy was exhausted from her all-nighter. With no leads, it was the perfect time to snuggle up and catch up on much-needed sleep.

The door slamming open woke the girls with a start. Arthur burst into the room with a determined, wild look on his face. Jane and Kennedy knew that look all too well. It was the look he got when he had discovered something and was trying to figure out the details of a case. He was oblivious to the world around him when he had that look. Case in point, he hadn't noticed that they had been sleeping.

"Jane, you were right," Arthur babbled that his words were almost squished into one. "He had booked everything in his ex-wife's name. The hotel, the conference hall, and when he was brought in, he was also booked in under her name. How they got away with that, I will never know. I guess his assistant paid off the administration staff. He's right here, in The Royal London Hospital," Arthur gushed, pacing the small room.

The news was huge; it meant the case was solved. They had found the missing billionaire, or had they? Something was still off. Arthur wouldn't have burst in so wildly if it were an open and shut case. Jane's gut twisted.

"Great, what's the hurry about, then? You found him," Jane could see the wheels in Arthur's head spinning.

Like Kennedy had theorised before, whatever was going on was much bigger than a missing person case. Was he in intensive care? Had someone tried to kill him? So many questions span in Jane's mind.

"He's in the morgue."

"What? He's dead?" Kennedy gasped.

A chance to meet her hero, to be involved in finding and saving him, ripped from her grasp. Jane could see the hurt in Kennedy's eyes, and she pulled her close.

CHAPTER 6

A dead billionaire in the same hospital Jane was staying in. This was incredible, almost unbelievable news. Kennedy hoped that they were the only ones to have figured this out. Once this story broke on the news, every amateur sleuth would be begging to help solve it. And the hospital would be swarming with paparazzi.

"What do we do?" Kennedy asked wide-eyed, still in shock. Her hero was dead.

"I'm going to pay a visit to my old friend, Dr Fitzpatrick. Care to join me, Kennedy?" Arthur looked over to Jane and frowned. "Sorry, Jane, but you're on bed rest."

Kennedy looked to Jane for guidance, and Jane smiled sweetly back at her, stroking her cheek. Kennedy nodded; she wanted to know what happened more than anything. She kissed Jane and left the room with Arthur.

"So, who is Dr Fitzpatrick? Another ex-roommate?" Kennedy asked, walking quickly, trying to keep up with Arthur.

Kennedy wasn't usually one for idle gossip but found she was pleased for any distraction at that moment.

"My ex-girlfriend, actually. She works here as a doctor. Her office is next to the morgue, so it seems she's the best person to talk to."

The lift down to the bottom floor was rickety and old. It wasn't used by anyone other than the hospital staff and the deceased. It was unsettling and sent a cold chill down Kennedy's spine. As the lift approached the bottom, the air became cooler, and the smell of strong sanitation and cleaning products filled the otherwise stale air.

The lift stopped with a slight thud, and the doors opened wide. There was a short hallway where the lights flickered; the bulbs were ready to give up on life too. Three doors lined the corridor, one on each side and one at the far wall. The small size surprised Kennedy. For a hospital the size of London Hospital, Kennedy expected the morgue to span an entire floor.

Arthur looked at every door; the far door was labelled *morgue,* and the other two were Rooms 188 and 189.

"Dr Fitzpatrick is in Room 189," he walked over to the door and knocked lightly. He had calmed himself down during their trip to the basement. Good, Kennedy thought. He'll approach this with a level head.

A beautiful woman with long blonde hair answered the door and smiled, welcoming Arthur and Kennedy into her office. She greeted Arthur with a warm hug and extended her hand for a shake with Kennedy.

"I'm Dr Fitzpatrick, but please call me Dannie," she smiled warmly. "Are you Arthur's wife?"

Kennedy and Arthur burst out laughing. They were great friends, sure, but Kennedy was deeply in love with and married to Jane, and Arthur was married to his job.

"No," Arthur shook his head, still chuckling. "This is Kennedy Daniels, a great friend of mine. And happily married to her wife, Jane."

Dannie's face flushed red. It wasn't the first time one of the Daniels had been asked if they were married to Arthur. Two women being married wasn't exactly unusual, but in a heteronormative society, strangers mostly assumed that they must be married to a man.

Kennedy watched Dannie and noted a small smile at the idea of Arthur being single. Kennedy couldn't help but smile when she realised that Arthur hadn't picked up on it either.

"Sorry about that, Kennedy. Such a pleasure to meet you," she paused and turned her head to look more closely at Arthur. "I know that look. What's going on?"

"Do you have a Mrs Norma Harris in the morgue right now?" Arthur was trying to act nonchalant, but it was clear that he had trouble hiding his emotions from Dannie. She made him nervous.

Dannie nodded and looked taken aback. Mrs Norma Harris was the name on the records, but the body lying in its place was a man, and Arthur shouldn't have had access to those records. Unless something was amiss, seeing as a man with a woman's name lay dead, was the case.

"Great. Have you performed an autopsy?" he questioned.

Shaking her head, Dannie told Arthur and Kennedy about their system's problems for the last couple of hours. She wasn't authorised to work until the system security was restored. She wouldn't do an autopsy unless there was an investigation into the patient's death, and they had the man's authentic details, and a next of kin had been informed.

Arthur looked sheepishly at Dannie.

"That was me, sorry. I tried looking through the more accessible database but couldn't find what I was looking for. I hacked the system," Arthur looked at Kennedy. "Kennedy here wouldn't have left any traces, so I probably should have let her do it, in retrospect."

"No worries, Arthur. To be honest, I had a suspicion that something like this might happen. It's unheard of that a man is booked in under a name not his own. On the records, the dead body belongs to Mrs Norma Harris, but I have no idea who lays in the morgue."

Arthur and Kennedy filled in Dannie about the case. Arthur asked questions about his stay at the hospital. When was he brought in? What was he treated for? And who fudged the records to hide his identity?

After digging into the hospital records, Dannie discovered that he had been in the hospital since New Year's Day. He was brought in after he broke his wrist in the hotel he was staying at while he was in London. A slip in the shower. That's why he was in the orthopedic ward next to Jane's room. His medications seemed normal for his symptoms, and he only had two nurses and one doctor providing him care – Dr Hamilton, nurse Mary, and nurse Juliette. They guessed the staff were paid to keep their mouths shut in case the paparazzi discovered he was there.

"And what is the official cause of death?" Arthur asked.

"I haven't done an autopsy, so there isn't one. I'll take a look and see what the chart says because, as of right now, that's the most official documentation," she walked over to her desk and pulled a file from a stack. Her desk was messy, but it looked like organised chaos as she quickly found the file.

"There isn't a cause listed, though it mentions some heart issues during his stay. Other than that, there's just a time and a signature from nurse Mary."

"Aren't nurses required to write more details than that?" interjected Kennedy.

Mary was Arthur's ex-flatmate, so she was concerned that his judgement could be clouded. She was also worried that Mary was Jane's nurse. Had the nurse been doing a good job of ensuring details about Jane's recovery were being kept? Proper documentation was essential and could be a big deal if there were complications. Or was she hiding something bigger? Was Jane in danger? Kennedy needed to know.

"Yes, they are. This report is bizarre… and cause for further investigation," Dannie said, clearly annoyed.

Kennedy could see the similarities and why Arthur was taken by her. Beauty aside, she was an intelligent woman and took her job as seriously as Arthur took his.

CHAPTER 7

Kennedy left Arthur and Dannie to go over more details about the case before Dannie could start the official autopsy. Kennedy wasn't a fan of blood and gore, so she chose to leave them be and fill in Jane about what they had discovered.

As she passed the room next to Jane's, yellow tape was being put over the door in the shape of an X. The investigation had officially started, and it wouldn't be long before the whole world knew about Albert's death.

"Jane, are you awake?" Kennedy opened the door slowly and poked her head in. Jane was sitting up in her bed and smiled at her.

"Yes, I can't rest without knowing more details. I have seen police officers walking past my room for hours. My mind is going crazy!" she laughed and beckoned Kennedy over to the bed.

"So, Dannie is Arthur's ex-girlfriend. Isn't that wild? I've never even thought about him dating. He loves his job too much to spend time getting to know somebody romantically."

Jane laughed and thought about how odd it would be to see Arthur with an ex-girlfriend.

"Was she beautiful? I feel like she would have to be gorgeous to catch his attention." Kennedy nodded.

"Skinny and blonde. A little stereotypical, if I'm honest."

"Enough about Arthur, now, what happened to Mr Candlestone? Is it case closed?"

Kennedy shook her head and walked over to the door to ensure it was shut tightly.

"There is some issue with the report. No autopsy was performed because there was no reason to do one; it was just a regular death. But the report that nurse Mary wrote had no details at all. There was only a time," Kennedy paused. "He was in the room next to yours. Your suspicions had been correct. If you hadn't been so insistent, we might never have found out what happened to him."

Jane's eyes widened. The shouting. Because it was still so foggy, she had no recollection of what was said and certainly wouldn't recognise the voices.

The girls brainstormed all the possible reasons for the shouting that they could. It could have been a mistress since he was so wealthy. He might have become violent to one of the staff if he was confused and overly medicated. What if Mary had witnessed the murder and been paid by the killer to keep quiet and cover it up? What if she had over-medicated him and covered it up out of fear? Or had one of his tech rivals found him and killed him?

"Hopefully, Dannie and Arthur can figure out what went wrong on the hospital side of things," Kennedy sighed.

Just then, the door swung open, and Jane's mum was standing in the door frame again. She smiled big and walked up to the girls.

"It's great to see both of you. I couldn't stay away. I had to check on my baby girl."

Jane was so thankful for her mum. It was great to see her again, and she was glad she had come a few times. She must have taken a lot of time off work. Jane chatted with her mum for a bit, but her mind was elsewhere. That is until Jane's mum brought up children.

"So, have you and Kennedy considered having children?" she smiled. "I'd love to be a grandma one day, you know."

Jane told her mum about their plans to look into IVF after failed donation attempts years ago, which halted their plans. It was too painful seeing the negative pregnancy tests month after month. They had agreed to look at other options but never had until now.

"Jane, you're going to be an amazing mum. I'm so happy for you."

A tear rolled down her mother's cheek.

* * * *

Arthur and Dannie studied the file and figured out that Mr Candlestone's symptoms at the end of his life were more accurately aligned to poisoning. Not natural causes at all.

"We need to get a court order to do an autopsy," Arthur nodded, and Dannie agreed.

"I'll get down to the station and talk to my team. I'm sure we'll be able to get an autopsy no problem. I should be back in a few hours," Arthur paused. "If you get a free moment or two, could you check on the Daniels? They're great people, and I trust them to be of assistance in my absence."

Upon exiting the hospital, he was greeted with fresh air. The sky was a bright blue, and a few fluffy clouds floated around. The temperature was cold, but it was January, and that was to be expected. After being inside the hospital for a while, he had gotten used to the stale air. Outside, he saw Mary sitting on a bench and smoking a cigarette.

"Mary, mind if I sit with you while I wait for a taxi?" Mary patted the bench next to her.

Arthur examined her closely. Her muscles were rigid, and she had deep purple circles under her eyes. She looked as though she had been crying. The Mary he knew didn't cry unless it was really bad. She was too analytical for emotions. He wondered what had happened and if it was related to the case. He dared not think Mary of such a thing as murder, but he had to be objective.

"How are you, Mary?" he asked.

"You know, the usual. We had a patient die yesterday, which is always hard," she sighed, not making eye contact with Arthur.

Mary took another long pull of her cigarette, blowing the smoke high into the air. Arthur had never known Mary to smoke; he wondered when she started. He couldn't figure out what Mary would have to do with a billionaire. Perhaps there was a medication mistake, an accidental double dose?

He was about to open his mouth to speak when a taxi pulled up. The streets were busy, and a few people were outside also eyeing the car. Somebody would get it first if he dawdled.

"I better get that," he looked at Mary. "I'll be seeing you later."

Mary waved him off dismissively, still refusing to make eye contact. Arthur's chest constricted. Could the sweet, caring Mary he knew from time ago be involved? Could she be a killer?

* ✳ ❋ ✳ *

Returning to find Jane and Kennedy asleep in Jane's bed, Arthur woke them gently. After all, he had news to share. The team got approval to make an autopsy request because Dannie had written a compelling letter stating that the report was sketchy and required an investigation.

The next step was to interrogate Mary and determine why there was a suspicious lack of details regarding Mr Candlestone's death. He still couldn't make sense of it. He had been toying around with the idea that she had forgotten to add a page to the file. If she had been on a double shift, it was possible.

"Kennedy, would you like to accompany me? We can do good cop bad cop," he looked down at his hands. "I'm not sure I can be too hard on her, and I'd appreciate your help."

Kennedy nodded. Mary walked in to take Jane's vitals as they were about to leave. Arthur turned to block Mary before she could get to Jane. Mary looked up at Arthur, surprise and horror plastered her face. Was it a sign of guilt?

"I'm going to have to ask you to come with us, Mary. We have a few questions for you," his voice was stern and firm – His detective's voice.

It wasn't harsh or meant to intimidate, just to set boundaries and ensure that she knew he wasn't talking to her as his old friend. He was talking to her as an officer of the law. Mary looked like a deer caught in the headlights.

"What is this about?" Mary stuttered.

"I think you know what this is about," Kennedy used her most intimidating voice, her eyes hard glaring Mary down.

"Follow us, please. This won't take long," Arthur added.

Arthur, Kennedy, and Mary walked through the hospital and went downstairs to Dannie's office. Kennedy loudly knocked on the door. It swung open, and Dannie stood there, looking stern.

"Come in," Dannie was the type to do everything by the book and took her job very seriously.

Knowing that she worked with a nurse who didn't care about adequately filling in reports was bad enough but knowing that one of her colleagues was suspected of poisoning a patient, let alone a billionaire, was even worse.

"Mary," she nodded curtly.

Dannie pulled a chair for her and walked around to her side of the desk. Arthur took a seat at eye level, and Kennedy stood next to him, staring down and glaring at Mary.

"Were you a nurse for a man brought in and booked under the name Mrs Norma Harris, a recently deceased patient?" Arthur asked calmly.

"Yes, I was," she nodded, not making eye contact.

"And how did he die?" Kennedy snapped.

She couldn't help herself; she had to know. And her job was to be a bad cop. She wanted to make Mary squirm. Kennedy had looked up to Mr Candlestone. He was a pioneer in the robotics industry and incredibly smart. His latest invention would make a massive difference in the lives of millions, and now he wouldn't get a chance to see it to fruition. It wasn't fair. She had hoped to meet him one day to talk about all his innovations and even share her love for him with her child.

"I don't know. He just died. I'm not a coroner."

Kennedy glared and put her hands down on the desk. "He just died?" The way she worded it was almost cruel. A man lost his life under her care; she was responsible for knowing why. And if she didn't, she was responsible for requesting an autopsy for further evaluation. Kennedy leaned forward to intimidate her and tried to make eye contact. Mary wouldn't look her in the eye, focusing on anything else in the room.

"So, he's a medical mystery? Do you know his real identity?"

Mary shook her head. She finally made eye contact with Kennedy. Her eyes were cold and malicious.

"I need to ask a few questions and take some notes, Mary. We'll be done soon. Can you tell me about your interactions with him in your own words? We want to compare everything to what you wrote in the patient's file."

When Mary was finished being questioned, Kennedy and Dannie looked at Arthur expectantly.

"Her story matches the notes. The only issue is that the story matches word for word. There's no variance. It was rehearsed," Kennedy said, frustration starting to set in.

CHAPTER 8

"Great news, guys! I get my crutches today. I can help in the investigation!" Jane grinned.

She was so excited to be able to join in on the sleuthing. And to meet Dannie, Arthur's ex-girlfriend.

"Are you sure that you're ready?" Kennedy asked, concerned. Jane could be a little overzealous and might have overestimated her ability to use crutches.

"Yes, I'm sure," she was still smiling.

The three of them chatted for a while, and Jane decided it was time to tell Arthur about her plans to become a private investigator. She thought it might explain why she was eager to be involved in this case.

His reaction was as expected; very supportive and excited. He couldn't wait to have Jane join him and Kennedy in their investigations. Right now, Jane was helpful and offered great ideas but didn't have Arthur's detective background or her wife's technological prowess.

Arthur's phone started ringing, and the caller ID showed that it was Dannie. The autopsy must be done.

"Alright, it's time to go talk to Dannie. Let's find out what the autopsy showed."

Getting to Dannie's office proved slower with Jane in toe. She was a little uneasy on her crutches but determined not to let them hold her back and to be involved in the case.

. ✳ ✳✳ ✳ .

"What are the results, Dannie?" Arthur cut to the chase.

"Albert Candlestone died of digoxin poisoning and from a bullet through the heart." Her face was white and scrunched up, trying to make sense of the results.

"So whoever killed him wasn't happy that the poison was taking so long and grew impatient," Arthur shook his head.

"Someone gave him an excessive dose of digoxin, which killed him relatively slowly. Maybe half an hour after ingesting the tablets. Then, the murderer decided to fire a small calibre gun into him point blank. Probably fitted with a silencer," she paused, taking in Kennedy and Arthur's faces. "Because his heart had already stopped, the blood stains were minimal and easily wiped up by the killer afterwards."

Kennedy and Arthur were in shock. Someone had gone so far as to kill Mr Candlestone. Was this a hit? Was it someone who didn't understand how digoxin worked? What could cause someone to hold so much hatred for another that they would resort to such measures?

"Do you have access to the visitor logs? Who was with him in the hour before he died?"

"Only nurse Mary, and his wife, Emily," Dannie shook her head sadly.

"I guess we need to question Emily, then. She's suspect number one at the moment. We can question Mary again, too, if we can rule Mrs Candlestone out."

CHAPTER 9

Arthur went to the precinct to share his findings with his team. They brought in Emily and questioned her, but she was clearly a sad widow with no helpful information to offer. She mostly cried and begged for them to find out who murdered him. She even blamed Mary, saying she was the worst nurse on his team. Plus, she had an alibi; CCTV put her in the hotel bar at the time of her husband's death.

Arthur and an accompanying officer entered the interrogation room where Mary had been waiting. She looked nervous and was fidgeting in her seat. She looked different when she wasn't wearing her scrubs. Her hair was pulled up into a neat high ponytail, and she wore a dark blue jumpsuit. Arthur was still in shock that she could have done something like this. She was always a sweet girl, a little wild, but had a good heart.

The room was cold and had double-sided glass, so the walls were just black. The seats and table were drilled into the ground so they couldn't be thrown, and there was a camera in the corner of the room pointed directly at Mary.

"Mary Hernandez, you're a nurse at The Royal London Hospital. How many patients have you worked with during your career?" the officer asked.

"I don't know," she shrugged.

"You're going to have to give us more details than that. A guess, even," Arthur looked at her sadly.

"A few thousand. I've been in nursing for fifteen years," she sat up a bit higher in her chair.

She was very proud of being a nurse, as healthcare professionals usually are. The only difference was that most healthcare workers weren't being investigated for the murder of one of their patients.

"And, Mary, have you ever not filled out the cause of death in a client's file before Mr Candlestone?" interjected the officer.

"No," she shook her head. "I always fill it out. I must have been tired, and I thought I would be able to write it during my next shift. By then, the file had already been given to Dr Fitzpatrick."

Mary was visibly uneasy, her knee bounced under the table, and her eyes darted around the empty room, searching for anything to focus on other than the officers in front of her. Her entire career was being questioned initially, but it was intentional. Though it was hard to drill someone about their passion and draw upon their insecurities, they wanted her to squirm so they could find out if she was the killer. The officer moved closer to her and looked her in the eyes.

"Are you familiar with the medication digoxin?" the officer asked.

"Of course I am," began Mary. "I wouldn't be much of a nurse if I didn't. It's used to treat heart conditions."

"We know you poisoned him, Mary."

Mary's eyes widened.

"We just want to know why," Arthur said.

"Did he say something to offend you?" the officer asked.

"No… it isn't like that," her eyes started to glisten, and her lips were trembling. "It wasn't Albert. It was Emily."

"Emily Candlestone, his wife?" Arthur and the officer exchanged looks. They had just spoken to Emily, and she had come across as being heartbroken and devastated. There wasn't a single word in that round of questioning that would have rung any alarm bells. They had already ruled her out of the suspect pool. "She's the one who shot him?"

"No, Arthur, that isn't what I'm saying," she was fully crying now.

"Emily is the one who offended me. I know this will come out one day, but Albert's will was changed to leave everything to me when he died."

"Bullshit, Mary. That's not true," snarled the officer. Were they expected to believe that he randomly decided to leave a nurse his entire fortune?

"It is true!" she shrieked. "I was in love with him, okay? We were in love." Mary was in full-blown hysterics, sobbing and shaking. Her whole body was rocking back and forth in the chair.

"We were having an affair. Together almost two years. I decided to break it off because I needed money, and he wouldn't give me any. I walked in on Albert and Emily arguing about how he had changed the will and knew I was running out of time. So I poisoned him."

Arthur was shocked. His old friend Mary was not who she used to be; she was a stranger to him.

"And after you poisoned him...?" the other officer wanted to figure out whether or not she was the one who shot him, too. She wouldn't have needed to shoot him if she had administered the lethal digoxin dose.

"When they were fighting, I went out for a cigarette. I saw Emily's car parked outside, and the doors were unlocked. She had a little gun in the glove box...and I took it...and shot him in the heart," she gasped. "Because he broke mine! I wouldn't have to do this if he left her."

Arthur was appalled at what he was hearing. She did murder him. He felt sick to his stomach.

"I loved him. You have to believe me," she pleaded. Arthur looked down at his hands, his heart heavy. Mary was a great friend. But he had nothing to offer her now, after what she did.

"Mary Hernandez, you're under arrest for the murder of Albert Candlestone. Whatever you do or say can and will be held against you in a court of law." Arthur grabbed Mary's arms and pulled them behind her back, clasping the cuffs on each wrist.

CHAPTER 10

Mary's trial was lengthy and highly publicised. Given Mr Candlestone's billionaire status, it was making global headlines. The tech industry, in particular, was in chaos. His business partners pushed forward with his biotech design while others tried to fight that he had stolen their ideas. With no Mrs Candlestone to fight his case, it made for compelling court room drama.

Kennedy and Jane were mostly left out of it; the only time Jane had to testify was to confirm that she heard yelling coming from the room the night Mr Candlestone died.

Arthur and Dannie had rekindled their romance. They were practically inseparable outside of working hours. Her assistance on the case was so greatly appreciated that Arthur had decided to take her to dinner. And then they went to another dinner and another...until they officially became a couple. He was happier than the Daniels had ever seen him.

While Jane's leg finished healing, the Daniels spent most of their time at home. Kennedy had started to review the requirements for IVF and the best hospitals. Jane had begun working on her private investigator licence. A lot of it could be done online, though she had a mentor who took her on stakeouts. They were working on a case of a wealthy woman trying to catch her husband cheating. That was the most common reason for someone to hire a PI these days; not as exciting as Jane had hoped, but still, she was happy. Putting together the clues and compiling evidence gave her a rush. Solving the mystery was so satisfying to her.

A few clients had approached Kennedy to upgrade their various business and software programs, giving Kennedy some extra spending money. They decided to put money aside to take a nice romantic cruise for Valentine's Day, which was right around the corner.

Through the stress of the trial, they had spent a lot of time together and had an even stronger bond. They didn't know that was possible. Much of their time was spent talking about their child's future. More importantly, who they would look like. They had decided to use the two-egg method, where an egg from Jane and an egg from Kennedy would be used. That way, it would be a surprise and take the stress of choosing away from them.

They still had to pick which one of them was going to be pregnant. But that conversation could wait until another day. Right now, they are content with their lives and their careers. Jane wanted time to finish her licence and work to save money, and Kennedy had dreamed about visiting Japan before their future child was born.

Life was good, and it would keep getting better—a New Year, a fresh start and the fun of not knowing what the future held.

The End

WHISPERS IN THE WINTER FROST

A MYSTIC MOONHAVEN MYSTERY

CHAPTER 1
FROSTY BEGINNINGS

As I fastened my nametag to my shirt, I couldn't help but reminisce. It had been a year since I uprooted my life to settle in Moonhaven, a decision driven more by instinct than reason. My new identity as Harper Nightshade, owner of the town's only occult bookstore, 'Nightshade's Nook,' felt as surreal as the mystical tomes lining its shelves.

The crisp winter air seeped through the cracks as I flicked on the radio, letting cheerful tunes displace the morning silence. Mondays were my sanctuary from the usual hustle–no regular hours, just me and my beloved store. Today, I planned to transform this sanctuary for the Winter Festival. Climbing the ladder, I reached for the 'Happy New Year' banner, but a sudden chill crept down my spine, an all-too-familiar frosty touch that spoke of unseen presences.

Heart pounding, I scanned the room, every shadow and corner. My shop, a cozy haven of ancient books and arcane artifacts, seemed unchanged, yet the air felt charged as if a whisper from the other world lingered just beyond my perception. I eyed the evergreen garlands and the small tree on the cashier's counter, remnants of a Christmas celebrated with my own blend of tradition and witchcraft.

The bell above the door jangled, snapping me back to reality. I spun around, losing my footing on the ladder. A scream escaped my lips as I braced for the fall.

Strong arms caught me, steadying me before I could hit the ground. I found myself looking into the concerned eyes of Detective Liam Ashford. His presence, unexpected yet oddly reassuring, sent a wave of heat to my cheeks.

"Are you alright, Harper?" His voice was laced with genuine concern.

"Yes, thank you, Detective." I managed to steady my voice, though my heart still raced–whether from the fall or his proximity, I couldn't tell. He removed his knitted hat, revealing the perfectly tousled hair that somehow added to his magazine-worthy appearance. "I noticed the lights on. Thought I'd check in." I nodded, feeling a mix of gratitude and embarrassment. "I'm redecorating for the festival. Should've locked the door, though."

"Speaking of which, be extra careful these mornings," he said, his tone shifting to professional concern. "We've had reports of wolves in town. And if you notice any strange people lurking around, let me know."

Wolves? In Moonhaven? The news sent another shiver through me, though this time, it wasn't from any spectral chill. "I haven't seen anything amiss. But something does feel off."

Liam raised an eyebrow, his usual skepticism surfacing. "You mean beyond wildlife concerns?"

"It's hard to explain. It's like a... frost in the air," I said, careful not to mention the spectral presence I had sensed. "A feeling that something is about to happen."

His smile was a blend of amusement and disbelief. "Mystical energy, Harper?"

"Maybe," I replied a little defensively. "There's more to this world than what we see. Sometimes, you have to trust your instincts."

He pondered my words for a moment, then nodded. "Just stay safe. And call if anything unusual comes up." As he headed for the door, the sense of an unseen presence faded, leaving me alone with my thoughts and a store in need of decoration. But Liam's visit had stirred something within me–a realization that my connection to Moonhaven ran deeper than mere chance. I resumed my task, my mind buzzing with questions and the frosty touch of the unknown still lingering at the edge of my awareness.

There was a palpable reason Moonhaven reserved its Winter Festival for the cruelest months of January. The relentless cold had a way of seeping into the soul, inspiring a kind of introspection that bordered on the mystical, even for those who didn't dabble in the occult.

I was pulled by these macabre thoughts by the door again. It swung open to reveal Abigail Thorne, her grey hair a silver crown beneath a hand-knitted hat. Her smile was a beacon in the frosty air, warming the room instantly.

"Ah, Detective! Always a pleasure," she greeted, wrapping Liam in a hug that spoke of a lifelong familiarity.

Out of everyone in town, Abigail was pretty much the only person who could get away with something like that. It helped that she owned the Bed and Breakfast that most newcomers end up staying at while they find a permanent place to live. I was still there, renting out a room at a much-reduced price. Unfortunately, the housing market in Moonhaven left much to be desired.

Liam had known her his whole life. He gave her an indulgent smile.

"It's good to see you, too," he told her. "I have to be on my way, though. I'll be by the B&B later to fix that leaking sink."

"You're a gem, Liam," she replied, her eyes twinkling with a mirth that seemed to know too much.

Liam left, and I shut the door after him, locking it.

"Things still seem to be frosty between you, too," Abigail noted.

I shrugged. "We just don't get along. It's one of those things."

"I always thought you two would get along famously."

Oh, she was fishing for information. I hesitated; the truth of everything seemed to be rather infantile whenever I tried to explain it out loud. I'd only told my best friend from Moonhaven, Ella. Abigail had tried to wheedle the information from me before, but I'd been closed-lipped.

I sighed. No point in holding onto the secret forever. "The day I had my grand opening, he called my store 'hooky' and said that I was peddling nonsense. I got mad at him and told him he was born under a bad sign, and he laughed. I don't even know why I said that."

Sure, he had no way of knowing I was a witch, but he insulted my livelihood. Nobody in town knew I was a witch. It was the one thing I had always been extra careful to keep a secret.

"He said that to your face?" Abigail asked, her eyes widening.

I blushed. "He didn't know I was the owner. And he apologized. But he's so practical. I like to act on my gut. So, we just can't get along."

I busied myself, taking down some decorations at eye level to avoid Abigail's gaze. She looked amused, which wasn't exactly the best sign. What was she thinking? I couldn't imagine anything good. She had a reputation in town for being a little eccentric.

"It doesn't matter, anyway," I blurted. "He was just here to ask if I'd seen anything weird. There are apparently wolves around. Or at least, people think they're seeing wolves."

I shrugged.

Abigail nodded once. "Just remember, frost is just the beginning, my dear."

A shiver ran down my spine. I turned toward Abigail fully, squinting. "What do you mean by that?"

Abigail chuckled and shuffled toward the door. "I think I'll head over to the coffee shop. A nice hot coffee will do just the trick to warm up these aching bones. I'll be out late tonight, dear. I'll have a casserole in the fridge that you can heat."

"Thanks," I said, frowning.

She gave me an enigmatic smile before she unlocked the door and strode toward the coffee shop across the street.

What was that about? Frost is just the beginning... Was it about the weird energy that is permeating Moonhaven or between Liam and me? Which, honestly, that had a lot of weird energy, too. I thought it must be because my magic was bouncing off and being repelled by his skepticism.

I locked the door behind Abigail. Eccentric, yes, but she was a kindred spirit. She was a wonderful person and had made me feel so welcome in the town when I first moved here. Which I desperately needed… I'd moved shortly after the deaths of my parents, using my inheritance to open up this store.

Even now, as much as I loved the town and my store, I would give anything to have my parents back.

The lights went out.

I jumped as a chill washed down my back again. The pale morning light filtered through the blinds, barely enough to light the interior of my store. I held my hand palm out and whispered an incantation. A flame jumped to life, warming my face.

Normal spirits can't interact with the world like turning off lights… was this a poltergeist?

"Alright, whatever you are," I called out. "I'm not interested in playing games. Turn the lights back on, or I'll have to get nasty."

My threat reverberated in the empty store. I headed for the front desk, observing anything that might fall on my head. Once I was there, I held the flame over the drawer, looking for the master switch for the lights.

Something caught my eye on the little Christmas tree. A man's face reflected in one globe. I gasped and leaned closer—

A wind burst through the shop, knocking books off the shelf. My flame blew out at once.

CHAPTER 2
A DISAPPEARANCE IN THE SNOW

The next day, instead of going straight to the bookstore, I headed to *Ella's Wheel*, the best coffee shop in Moonhaven. I had to say it was the best, because my best friend, Ella, was the owner of the place. It was the best, though, even if I might be biased.

Ella must have seen the cloud hanging over my head as I took my normal seat, frowning. She slid a sugar cookie to me.

"I'll be back soon," she promised me. "I have a couple of other orders to fill first."

I nodded at her. "Take your time. I'm in no hurry."

I spun the cookie on the plate. Normally, I'd jump at the opportunity to eat sugar for breakfast, but today, I was too involved in the events that happened yesterday. Who was the spirit I'd seen in my bookstore, and why was he here?

The building was new, so it couldn't be a long-dead person emerging. Maybe he was drawn to the bookstore by the energy of my magic? That didn't explain the cold and how the lights went out, though. Spirits usually can't do that sort of thing.

There was something weird happening, and I didn't like it.

Ella returned to me and handed me a large cup of coffee prepared just the way I liked it.

"Did you know him?" she asked me with a sympathetic look.

I frowned at her. "Who?"

"David Blackwood. He's been reported as missing."

"What? When?"

I'd never met him personally, but it seemed like everyone around town knew him. He ran the museum and archives. I'd seen quite a few newspaper articles about various books he published on the history of Moonhaven and the people who lived here.

"This morning. Apparently, his roommate hadn't seen him for a few days and got worried when he didn't answer his phone," Ella told me, lowering her voice slightly. "Detective Liam found his car at the museum. It was still covered in that snow we got a few days ago."

I shivered as I processed this information. How horrible would it be to be missing for days and have nobody realize it?

"If his car was at the museum, where is he?" I asked.

Ella shook her head. "Nobody knows. That's why he's missing. There's no way to know if someone kidnapped him or if he got lost in the forest."

"Or maybe the books finally ate him," a voice on my other side said.

I turned to see Percival Whitman sitting there, looking amused. The Whitmans were the closest thing Moonhaven had to royalty. They were one of the founding families of the town and still owned over half of the property here. Percival had never worked a day in his life; all his income came from renting out the land to farmers and shop owners.

I was fortunate enough to own the store. Otherwise, I'd be paying the slimeball through the nose to stay in business.

"It's a wonder we even noticed he was missing," Percival drawled. "That nerd would stay in the museum for weeks at a time. Was never late for rent, though, so who am I to complain?"

Ella sighed. "Is that a subtle reminder that my rent is coming up due, Percy?"

"Not at all." Percival gave her a toothy grin. "I don't care if you're late, Ella. Where else am I going to find such delicious coffee than what you brew?"

I rolled my eyes at the obvious flirting. Ella wasn't interested in

Percival, but that didn't stop him. Luckily, he seemed to be content to keep it at flirting, but I already told Ella that we could put an addition on my bookstore for a new coffee shop if she wanted to.

"We're all hoping that Detective Liam will find David soon," Ella said, refilling Percival's mug.

"Of course, of course," Percival said.

He waved a hand and sauntered away.

Ella released a heavy breath and focused on me again. "Anyway. From what I've heard, David might have been in over his head in some financial crisis. Some people say that he faked his death to escape a debt he owes to the mob."

"That doesn't seem very likely." I sipped at my coffee, frowning. "Do you have a picture of him? I'm not sure I know what he looks like."

"Of course. Here." Ella whipped her phone from her apron pocket and started scrolling on it.

After a few minutes, she handed it to me. She had pulled up the museum website. Right at the bottom was a picture of David Black-wood. He had kind eyes and a solemn expression as he clasped a book to his chest.

I gasped.

It was the same man I'd seen in my bookshop yesterday. Dread filled me. Did that mean that David was dead? Had he sought me out to help find his body and bring him to peace?

"What's wrong?" Ella asked, peering around the counter at the frown. "Did one of my fanfic tabs open instead?"

I forced out a laugh at her joke and handed her the phone back. "Sorry. No, I just realized I know him. It's just so unnerving, you know? When this happens to someone you know."

It wasn't a great excuse, but it was the only one that I could think of. Nobody knew I was a witch. Ever since I was a kid, my parents drilled it into me that nobody could know. Even if these days witches were thought of in a generally more positive light than, say, the sixteen-hundreds, it was still dangerous to let anyone know.

My stomach curled around the little bit of coffee I'd put into it.

He wasn't just missing. He was dead. And he was coming to me for help. What could I do, though? I wasn't an investigator. Even if I found his body, how would I tell Liam about it? He'd probably think I was a suspect!

On the other hand, I had to do something. I hated the thought of David's spirit being lost in the cold like this.

"I wish I could get into the museum and look around," I said aloud. "Maybe I could help Liam somehow."

Percival spoke up again, proving he'd been eavesdropping on us still. "I have a key. It's my land and my building, after all. Here." He fished a keychain from his pocket, detached one, and handed it to me. "I'd like to see David back safe and sound, too."

"Thanks." I tucked the key into my pocket.

Ella shot me a 'be careful' warning look before she was called away. I wished I could bring her with me, but she was busy. I finished my coffee and headed out.

The museum was empty, as expected, when I arrived. I unlocked the front door and stepped in. A blast of icy air hit me, and I sucked in a hard breath. It was colder inside the museum than it was outside! I pulled my cap down over my ears and stepped in, looking around cautiously.

The sound of a car crunching the snow in the driveway made me spin. Liam's sleek cruiser pulled up and stopped. Even before he got out of the car, he frowned at me.

"What are you doing here?" he demanded when he joined me at the entrance.

"Percival Whitman gave me a key," I said, holding it up as proof. "I thought maybe I could help."

Liam pulled off his hat and ran his fingers through his hair. "This is the last thing I need—a bunch of hicks mucking up my investigation."

I stiffened. "Hicks?"

"Sorry. I didn't mean it like that." He actually looked abashed, which eased my indignation. "Only if Whitman goes around giving keys to whoever asks, that means my list of suspects is blown wide open."

I looked at the key in my hand. "He just gave it to me at the coffee shop. Ella has cameras if you need to check."

Liam shook his head. "You aren't a suspect, Harper. Just don't interfere in my investigation."

"I can help."

"You don't have the training."

I put my fists on my hips. "And maybe you rely too much on your training. There's such a thing as intuition, you know."

Liam's frown deepened. The tension simmered between us like a pot of water ready to boil. Finally, he waved his hand at the museum's interior.

"Alright, you can look around. Don't touch anything. If you see anything that looks out of place, take a picture and then find me. Got it?"

I nodded. "Yes, sir."

Liam rolled his eyes, but it looked like he was fighting a laugh.

He headed across the room to turn on the thermostat, and I held my hand out, palm-up. Watching to make sure Liam wouldn't catch on, I whispered a spell, calling on my searching wind. A breeze picked up around me, tugging at my hair. To anyone else, it would look like I was standing in a draft.

I followed the wind to behind David's desk. There, on the floor, was a single brass button.

"I found something," I called.

"Already?" Liam asked, sounding startled.

"There's a button on the floor here." I whipped out my phone and snapped a picture.

Liam came over, putting on latex gloves. He snapped a picture as well before he picked up the button. As he turned it this way and that, it caught the lights.

David's face flared on the brassy surface. His eyes were enormous, and his mouth moved as though he was shouting something.

An icy wind hit me in the square of my back, and I gasped.

Liam caught my elbow. "What's wrong?"

His eyes skimmed through the museum, searching for what set me off. I was so shocked at the protectiveness that he displayed that I forgot to answer at first. I only gaped at him as though that wasn't suspicious at all.

When he finally met my gaze again, he arched one of his brown eyebrows at me. "What's wrong?" he repeated.

"Nothing," I said, rolling my shoulders to lose the tension in them. "There was just a sudden shivery feeling. I guess the furnace must be pushing out the cold air."

Liam studied me like he wasn't sure if he believed me.

I cleared my throat, blushing. Even if I told him about what I just saw, he wouldn't believe me. Just knowing that tempted me to blurt out everything, but that wouldn't help. I needed to get back to town and see if I could contact David's spirit directly. It was clear he wasn't just hanging around my shop now.

Something bigger than a disappearance was happening here.

"I think you're right; I shouldn't be poking around here," I said, stepping backward toward the door. "I don't want to do anything that might jeopardize your case."

If I could contact David, though, I'd nudge Liam in the right direction. Right now, however, poking around the museum was a bad idea.

"On the other hand, you know now that Percival Whitman will hand out keys willy-nilly," I added. "I'm sorry for taking up your time."

Liam grabbed my hand before I could leave. He squeezed lightly, making goosebumps break out along my arm.

"Take care of yourself, Harper," he told me.

I smiled, touched by his concern. "I will. Promise."

. ✳ ✸ ✳ .

I spent the rest of the day trying to contact David's spirit without success. This whole thing was super frustrating. David had come to me twice already, yet when I tried to contact him, nothing. It only proved that something weird was happening. But what? I still had no idea.

I plopped onto the couch next to Ella, sighing heavily. I was exhausted from my repeated attempts to contact David, so I was glad she was here and giving me an excuse to get some downtime.

"Are you okay?" she asked me, a crease furrowing her brow.

"Tired. I've been feeling off all day," I told her.

Ella nodded as she flicked through our saved movies. "Do you want to reschedule, then?"

"No. A couple of rom-coms is exactly what I need," I told her. "But remind me tomorrow I need to finish putting up those garlands that the town gave me for the winter festival. I'm looking forward to the parade. I think the fireworks are going to help take the frost out of the air."

Ella selected a movie we'd previously decided on. "Yeah, it's always a lot of fun. January is rough, and this year, it's rougher. Detective Liam found a button in the museum, but so far no news about who the killer is."

I shuddered. "Let's not talk about that."

"Sorry."

Abigail bustled into my room, carrying with her a tray of finger food. She set it down on the coffee table and took up her usual spot in the chair. "What are we talking about, dears?"

"The Winter Festival," I answered.

"Ah. Terrible that it's being overshadowed by this dreadful business." Abigail shook her head. "I still have faith that dear David might be found alive."

I had to look away.

"We're trying not to talk about that," Ella told Abigail. "Hey, did you know that the Winter Festival started because of a local folktale? That's why it happens in January in the middle of winter rather than at the start of winter."

Grateful for the distraction and always eager to learn more about it, I leaned forward. "Oh? What's the tale."

Abigail made a tutting noise. "Now, I'm not sure we should dredge up the old legends. Sometimes these things are made more powerful by talking about them."

I turned, wanting to ask what she meant, but before I could, Ella laughed.

"What powers? It's just a story. It all happened in sixteen-sixteen, ten years after Moonhaven was founded. It started with mysterious disappearances; people snatched out of their homes in the dead of night with no trace of them left behind," Ella said, lowering her voice.

Disappearances like David Blackwood.

"Then the bodies popped up. It was clear from the wounds that a ravaging pack of wolves was wandering the area, killing anyone in their path. The town grew frantic to protect themselves and set traps, but they were set off at night with no tracks around. Talk of an evil spirit in the area flourished."

"Oooh, I don't like this," I said anxiously. "Yesterday, Liam told me that people were seeing wolves around town."

Ella looked mildly interested. "Did he? When did you talk to him?"

"He came to her store," Abigail said. "I saw them when he left. They seemed to have a very close discussion."

"Oh?" Ella looked thrilled.

I shook my head. "Just finish the story."

Abigail sighed as she sipped her tea.

"Right." Ella cleared her throat. "Anyway. It all culminated in the disappearance of Penelope Whitman."

My eyes widened. "Whitman?"

"Yeah. She was the wife of whoever founded Moonhaven. I forget his name. Percival is a direct descendant of Penelope."

I processed that information. It seemed important, but how? I already knew that the Whitmans had founded Moonhaven. Maybe the museum held something that belonged to Penelope Whitman? It might be a connection.

"Anyway, after Penelope Whitman disappeared, all the strange things in town stopped. There were no more disappearances or deaths," Ella said, leaning back on the couch. "They found and trapped all the wolves in the area, too."

"Oh. That's a bit of an anti-climatic ending," I said.

Ella shrugged. "That's the story. She disappeared, and everything stopped. So, people ran around saying that she was a witch and caused it all. Especially after the witch hunts started in Salem."

I winced hard at that. I couldn't verify, since I didn't have the records of other witch families, but I doubted there were even any witches in Salem. Besides that, I wasn't sure I liked the casual way Ella was talking about it. As though Penelope deserved what she got just because she might be a witch.

There was a reason 'don't tell anyone' was drilled into me from before I said my first word.

Abigail snorted. "Ridiculous."

"What is?" Ella asked.

Abigail set her cup aside and skewered Ella with a no-nonsense look. "It's ridiculous to think that Penelope was a witch who started the whole thing just because it stopped when she disappeared. Those people. Didn't it occur to them that her wicked husband did away with her?"

"But there's no sign that he didn't love her," Ella protested.

"And who do you think wrote those history books, Ella? He did, that's who. Why would he talk about hating his wife?" Abigail shook her head hard, her wispy grey hair fluttering about her. "No. No, it's just like people to blame the victim for causing everything."

Ella shrugged. "I never thought she was a witch. I bet that it really was wolves. People went running around the countryside and got taken by wolves, or they got lost, or whatever. Winter is harsh, it doesn't need supernatural help. But I don't see why we should jump to Penelope being murdered by her husband, either."

Abigail snorted as she picked up her mug again. "It's because she was the one who owned everything, not him. Not to mention he remarried in a matter of months."

It looked like the two of them were winding up for a good argument. Not that either was a firm believer in what they said. Ella and Abigail liked to have debates. They'd argue over what I thought were silly things, but for them, it was about making themselves see from a new point of view. It was all in good spirits for them.

I didn't want to be caught in the middle of it tonight, though.

"I wonder if this has anything to do with David Blackwood," I wondered aloud.

Ella gave me a funny look. "It can't have anything to do with him. It's just a story about how the festival started. Now we have lights, and people are all out to frighten the wolves away from the town. It's just a coincidence that he disappeared at the same time."

Oh, but there was no such thing as coincidence when magic was concerned. I kept my expression smooth, and Ella started the movie. My mind kept racing over everything, though, and I couldn't settle. So, when my phone rang, I didn't even mind. I pulled it from my pocket.

"Hello?"

"It's Percival Whitman. You still have my key to the museum," he said. "I need you to meet me there right away."

CHAPTER 3
MIDNIGHT WHISPERS

"Don't go," Abigail said.

I stuffed my phone back into my pocket. "I have to go. It sounded important."

And maybe with Percival instead of Liam, I'd be able to get more answers. Liam was too sharp-eyed. With Percival, I might call on David's spirit and better find out what happened. I grabbed my keys with Ella and Abigail following close after me.

"It will do you no good to get mixed up with him," Abigail insisted. "At least call the detective and let him know what's happening."

I frowned at her. "You're talking as though Percival is going to hurt me."

"I never said that. But my bones are creaking, and there's frost out there. It's best to be wary and wise," Abigail said.

Was she trying to give me a hint? I searched her face, unable to read her. She seemed to be genuinely worried. Did she know something that I didn't? I chewed my lower lip. I really felt like I needed to go, but Abigail was right in that it wasn't exactly the smartest thing to do, to race out into the night when there was something out there that was causing trouble.

"I'll go with you," Ella said. She already had her coat on, her expression determined. "I can see on your face that you're going to go, even if you're unsure. So, I'm coming, too, and I'm bringing bear spray."

I smiled gratefully at her. Abigail didn't seem to be assayed but didn't argue with us any further.

"I'll call you in half an hour," I promised her and set the alarm on my phone as proof.

"Be careful, Harper," she warned.

Ella and I headed out. We reached the museum shortly to find all the lights on inside and the door wide open. Percival Whitman's car sat in the parking lot, the engine idling.

"Bear spray out," Ella said, holding the canister ready to spray.

She eyed the surrounding darkness nervously as we made our way to the museum. When I stepped through the door, I gasped. Percival Whitman lay face-down in the center of the room. His hair was matted around a nasty, bleeding injury.

I ran to his side. "Ella, keep a lookout."

She hurried to stand next to us, keeping her back to the wall while she watched the displays nervously. "Do you think they're still here?"

"I don't know."

I touched Percival's skin. He was still warm, so I picked up his hand gently and pressed my fingers to his wrist. His heart pounded. I released a heavy breath of relief.

"He's alive. Call Liam while I check for other injuries."

Ella reached into her pocket one-handed. I thought of the first-aid training I'd gone through and carefully swept my hands beneath Percival's body, checking for further bleeding injuries. With a head injury, I didn't want to move him in case we might damage him further.

"I don't have a signal," Ella said.

The wind howled, slamming the door shut. The windows rattled. Then the wind died, leaving us in an eerie silence—and a bitter cold. My breath puffed out visibly as I went to the door. It was stuck. Ella stood guard near Percival, so I whispered a spell—only for it to bounce off the door and disappear in a puff of smoke.

Nerves swept through me. There *was* magic happening here!

"The furnace isn't kicking on," I said as I lifted my hand to a nearby vent. "It didn't seem to work earlier, either. Let's see if we can start a fire."

"Isn't that dangerous?" Ella asked anxiously.

I shook my head grimly. "We'll freeze if we don't."

She shuddered. It didn't take long to search the small museum. To our relief, no attackers were hiding in the basement or archives. We found an old metal stove and dragged it up to the office space, setting it near Percival. There were also several old clothes and blankets we used to cover him up; he was getting cold, though his heart was still steady.

Neither of us wanted to burn anything important, so we dug into the recycling bins and found scrap paper. I sent Ella to the basement looking for matches, then whispered a fire spell and set our bounty ablaze.

"I found some matches in David's desk," I yelled down to her.

Ella returned, wrapping her arms around herself. "It's so cold."

We both sat near the stove, twisting the paper into tight rolls so they would burn slower. We quickly went through all the recycling. Frost covered the windows and crept over the sills. I didn't like the look of it.

"Still no signal," Ella said, pacing back and forth with her phone in hand.

I looked at my phone. The bars were empty, but the alarm I'd set for Abigail was still ticking down. How long after the allotted time would she wait before she got nervous? I added another twist of paper —and then jumped up as Ella screamed.

She'd put her hand on the windowsill, and the frost crawled up her skin. I raced over to her, but I was too late. The frost crept up over her face, and she collapsed, her eyes rolling to the back of her head.

"Ella!" I cried, catching her. I nearly dropped her, but dragged her closer to the stove.

The frost melted off her, but she remained cold and unconscious. Her breathing was deep and even, though, and her heartbeat was steady. I added more paper to the flames, then held both my hands upward and conjured my flames.

The frost retreated a little, then crept forward again. It spread past the windowsills and under the door, reaching icy fingers toward us.

"Harper Nightshade," a voice whispered.

I jumped and turned. There, on the far wall, a face emerged in the frost. My heart hammered; it was David! His eyes rolled and roved, as though he was in deep pain.

"Who did this?" I cried. "David, who killed you?"

"Beware the wolf in the wind," he whispered, and his face contorted as though each word was painful. "Search the Whitman words. They hold the key."

"Whitman words?" I repeated.

David howled and vanished.

What did he mean? Maybe he left notes? I raced to his desk and extinguished the flames on my hands. I searched through the drawers and finally found an old book. It was worn and delicate, and written by hand. I turned to the first page and read: *This is the journal of Penelope Whitman, 1615.*

Howls rose all around the museum. My head snapped up, and I clutched the journal to my chest. The breath left my lungs. There, in the frost covering the wall, a pair of glowing orange eyes glared at me. A wolf emerged from the frost.

It snarled, eyes locked on me.

The door banged open, and I screamed.

I readied myself to conjure a wind to defend myself with when Liam came in, holding a tazer in one hand. His dark eyes scanned the room before locking on me.

I shook hard as I stood there, my eyes wide. The wolf had disappeared the moment Liam entered. The frost melted at once, leaving only the barest trace on the windows. The temperature rose several degrees.

"Harper, are you okay?" Liam asked as he strode forward.

I swayed on the spot, suddenly exhausted. I braced myself on the desk. "Percival and Ella need the hospital."

"Let's get you out; I'll come back for them." Liam put an arm around my shoulders and helped me to the car, then went back in and carried out first Ella, then Percival. Percival helped to walk himself out;

it seemed he was getting some consciousness back. But as soon as he was in the car, he groaned and fell back to sleep.

When Liam pulled out of the parking lot, I saw a vague canine shape in the shadows of the trees, watching us. But it was gone before I could get a closer look.

"How did you know to come?" I asked as I slumped into my seat.

"Abigail called me," he replied. "You shouldn't have come out here like this, Harper. You could have been hurt."

I shook my head slowly. "If I hadn't, then wouldn't Percival have been killed? Ella and I must have scared off the attacker."

Liam's lips thinned. "The door was locked from the outside. Whoever did this wasn't scared off. I also smelled gasoline around the place. They were planning on burning it down, with the three of you inside."

A shudder raced down my spine. But even so, it made little sense. Why would someone go through that much trouble and also send the frost after us? I held my arms tighter around the book, pressing it into my ribs. The answer was here, somewhere. But I was far too tired to figure it out.

My vision darkened. I was going to pass out. Swallowing hard, I pushed the journal into Liam's lap.

"It holds the key," I told him. But he wouldn't believe David told me, so I added, "The desk was open, this was on the floor. Percival must have interrupted the attacker trying to steal it."

Then the darkness overwhelmed me, and I slumped against the cold window. And the last thing I heard was Liam calling my name.

CHAPTER 4
CHILLING REVELATIONS

I woke up warm and cozy in a hospital bed. Liam sat on a chair beside my bed, his eyes closed as he rested his head back against the wall. Surprise flooded through me, followed swiftly by a warmth in my chest. How long had he been sitting here, watching over me?

He stirred as I watched him, and I quickly looked away so he wouldn't know. Liam yawned, stretching his arms over his head. When he focused on me, I smiled up at him.

"You're awake." He grinned at me. "How do you feel?"

"Fine," I answered honestly.

Liam rested a hand on the bed next to mine. "No lingering headache?"

I shook my head. "What about Ella and Percival? Are they okay?"

"Yes. Both of them are still unconscious but they'll be fine. You were all very lucky."

I frowned at his tone. His face was pinched with worry, and I shook my head again, tracing back through my memories. Why would he say that? Was there another attempt at the museum? Or was there something else…?

"Did you find David Blackwood?" I asked him.

"No." His expression grew grave. "What happened? Tell me everything. You kept talking about a wolf all the way to the hospital."

"I was?"

Liam combed his fingers through his hair. "You were delirious, but it sounded important."

I bit my lip. How much could I actually tell him without him thinking I was crazy? But he needed to know everything, didn't he? I couldn't tell him about my magic, but if I told him about everything else... I sighed as I started from when Ella and I arrived and went through detailing everything.

Knowing him and his practicality, he'd come up with an explanation for it.

"Then, after David disappeared, and I found the journal, a wolf stepped through the frost. I knew it was going to kill us all." I shuddered as I remembered those deadly orange eyes. "You broke the door down, and it disappeared."

Liam's brows were lifted almost to his hairline. But he didn't call me crazy. Instead, he nodded slowly. "That explains it."

I chewed my lip again. Did he believe me?

I needn't have worried.

"When I looked through the museum again, I found the furnace was turned on, leaking gas into the building. You three were all suffering carbon monoxide poisoning. You hallucinated the whole thing," he said. His tone was clearly meant to be soothing.

Leaking gas? But we had a fire in that little stove. If we'd been subjected to carbon monoxide, wouldn't the whole place have lit up? No, whoever attacked Percival and locked Ella and me in the museum must have snuck in after we'd left to set the stage.

I couldn't help but flinch as I thought of whoever it was, watching and waiting for us.

Liam leaned forward, his expression worried. "Do you need a doctor?"

"No. It's just scary to think of," I blurted.

A knock came on the door. Abigail stepped through and beamed when she saw I was awake. She carried a thermos in one hand, a tightly wrapped bundle under her elbow. She hurried over to the bed and set them down on my nightstand.

"Oh, my dear! I'm so happy to see that you're alright," she said, hugging me tightly.

"Thank you for calling Liam. We wouldn't have made it out if you hadn't," I told her fervently.

Abigail released me and stepped back. Her smile faltered as she cupped my face in her hands. "Didn't I tell you not to go? Didn't I say Percival Whitman would be up to no good?"

"He was attacked," I protested. "When Ella and I came in, we found him with a nasty blow on the back of his head."

"Did he?" Abigail's eyes widened.

I nodded and then encouraged her to take a seat. "If we hadn't gone, he might have died. But everything worked out this time. I just wish we could have found something that would lead us to David."

Liam stood up. "Speaking of, I should go back to my investigation. Whoever did this has to have left clues at the museum. I need to do a more thorough look."

"But by this time, the attacker would have cleaned up after themselves," I said.

"I had a deputy standing guard."

I nodded, then spied the journal beneath his arm. "Oh! Let me see that. The journal."

Liam held it out to me. "I was going to leave it here, anyway. I don't know what's so special about it, it's just an old journal."

"I told you, I found it on the floor," I said, remembering my lie. "So, someone was interested in it. And it's Penelope Whitman's journal, too."

Abigail's eyes widened but Liam just looked confused. Right, he wasn't part of the discussion about how the Winter Festival got its start. That was definitely something he would not accept. He'd think it was just a coincidence, and I'd pushed my luck too much already.

I turned the book over in my hands, studying it. David had led me to it for a reason. But why?

A strange lump in the binding caught my eye. I pressed my fingers over it, to find something hard in a strange shape. Carefully, I pressed the flaps of the book backward, making the binding bend slightly. A key fell out of the spine, landing in my lap.

"What's that?" Abigail asked, leaning forward.

"It looks new." I studied it. "Maybe for a safe? David must have put it in there... maybe this is what the attacker was looking for?"

I reached for it, but Liam caught my wrist. "There might be prints."

He put on a glove and carefully picked it up, dropping it into a small plastic baggy. Then he sealed it and tucked the key into his jacket.

"Do you think it will help?" I asked him.

"I don't know. With any luck, it will. We have no prints to go on, yet."

He gave me a searching look. Not suspicious, but like he knew there was something more about this whole situation than I was letting on. I longed to know exactly what he was thinking. If he didn't suspect me as the attacker, what did he think I knew? Was he suspicious about why I was involved in the case?

Or was there something else? Had I been too reckless, telling him about what I saw in the museum?

"I'll check on you later," Liam told me.

"Thanks." I blushed. It was sweet that he'd do that for me when our relationship thus far hadn't exactly been friendly.

But Liam wasn't a regular sort of person. He genuinely cared about others. He was only looking out for me because he felt like he needed to protect everyone in town, and I was one of the few unfortunates who had been in danger lately. He would check in on Ella and Percival too, I was sure.

Once he was gone, Abigail pulled a tin of cookies from the bundle she brought. "These are for you. They'll get you on your feet in no time."

"Thanks," I said, grinning at her.

"I'm going to go sit with Ella for a bit. The poor thing hasn't woken up yet," Abigail said. She patted my hand. "I'll be right across the hall."

I nodded once at her and settled down to read. I felt fine, but it'd probably be good to give myself a bit more time. Besides, David told me to read the Whitman words. There had to be a clue in here, besides the key.

I opened the book and read the first line again. There was something off about Penelope's name. It seemed smudged somehow. I frowned at it for a while before I kept reading. I skimmed the first few pages until a name caught my eye.

My brother, Jeremiah Blackwood, disappeared today. They say there were wolf tracks around his homestead. There haven't been wolves in the area for years now. I worry that this is linked to my cousin's death last year, but nobody will listen to me. It's just a coincidence, they say.

Penelope was a Blackwood by birth? So, she must be distantly related to David. I turned the page and my eyes widened.

Howard Whitman came to ask for my hand again today. He's always asking in secret and begs me not to tell anyone. He makes me feel uneasy. His mother has invited me to come stay in their townhouse since Papa was killed by the wolves. I don't want to live with the Whitmans. I'll take my chances with the frost. Howard is just as cold and I swear I have seen him walking with wolves at night.

My heart pounded harder as I kept reading. When did she change her mind? Or was there another Whitman that she married? As I read, the air left my lungs. Every person who disappeared were relatives of Penelope.

And all their land, which totaled more than half of the properties in and around Moonhaven, all ended up going to her.

So that's how the Whitmans ended up owning the land. Whichever Whitman Penelope married, inherited it as her widower.

Only...

I turned back to the first page again.

Only, if she was rejecting Howard Whitman's proposals later on, why was her name Whitman on the first page?

It all clicked at once why her name looked smudged. Because someone had scrubbed out what she actually wrote and placed the Whitman name over it. My hand pressed to my mouth as I realized what this meant. Penelope Blackwood never married a Whitman.

Which meant all the Blackwood land should have belonged to David, not Percival.

CHAPTER 5
FESTIVAL OF FEARS

Abigail was still with Ella but didn't know where Percival's room was. When I went to the nurse's station, they told me he had checked himself out of the hospital an hour ago. Blood rushed in my ears as the pieces kept falling into place.

I dashed to my car and called Liam. If anyone could help me figure this out and stop Percival, it was him.

"Liam," I blurted as soon as he answered. "It was Percival Whitman. It was him all this time. David Blackwood uncovered proof that the Whitmans stole the Blackwood land."

"You might be onto something," Liam replied. "I'm at the museum now. That key you found didn't have any prints, but it unlocked a safe here. It's full of documents and property deeds in the Blackwood and Whitman names. David must have spent months researching this."

I started my car and pulled out of the hospital parking lot. Where would Percival have gone?

"David must have confronted him about it. Maybe he was giving Percival a chance to do the right thing, or maybe just giving him the heads up that he'd be revealing all of it to the public," I said as I drove toward Main Street. "Percival had a key to the museum. He could have easily snuck in and attacked David."

And if his ancestor had magic wolves, it followed to reason that Percival was a wolf, too.

There was the sound of a metal door closing and Liam's breathing became harder, like he was rushing up a set of stairs. "Where are you?"

"Looking for him," I said.

"Get back to the hospital. Don't you see what this means? He wasn't unconscious in the museum when Ella and you showed up. He set the scene to make it look like he'd been attacked," Liam said, sounding urgent. "He must have set it all up to lure you in. But he didn't know about the gas leak, which knocked him out before he could lock you and Ella into the museum and light it on fire."

Not exactly… he used his ancestral magic to bring the frost and the wolves in, then must have gone back to set the furnace leaking. Nobody would suspect him when he was unconscious in the hospital, after all. He'd put it all together perfectly. The one thing he hadn't expected was that Liam would arrive right in time to stop it.

He used the same tactics as his ancestor, the one who had forged a marriage to Penelope and then killed her to steal all of her land. But what was his plan? If it was just about preventing David from telling the truth about what happened four hundred years ago, he wouldn't have continued all of this… which meant he had other plans.

The festival? Was he planning to use the energy of everyone coming together to do something?

Howard Whitman, all those years ago, attacked many, many people. He put the blame on Penelope to divert suspicion even though he was the one who would profit… Percival had to be planning something similar. He was going to attack more victims to muddy the waters and make it seem like he wasn't part of it at all.

"Harper," Liam said urgently. "Go back to the hospital. Tell them what's happening. He'll go after you again."

I tightened my hands on the wheel. "If he does, he won't know what hit him."

The phone went dead. My heart jumped to my throat as I twisted to stare at it. At first, I thought we were wrong and Percival had gone after Liam—then I realized the signal bars were empty.

My car skidded and I pumped the brakes, my breath exhaling in puffs of white. When I finally stopped, I threw open the door. The road was slick with frost. I scrambled out of the car and leaped onto the sidewalk.

The frost crept up over my car and toward the center of town. A chill ran down my spine—no, it wasn't just about me and Ella in the museum. That was to set himself up as a victim. But this? This was so much bigger… He would not have a single attacker anymore.

It was the wolves. Percival Whitman was bringing the wolves to town. He was going to have a bloodbath, so nobody would even think about what had happened. He must have changed his plans the moment I gave Liam Penelope's journal, knowing that we'd figure out what had happened so far.

Fog rose from the frost. A figure appeared in the fog, moving away from me. My blood rushed in my ears as I took up the chase, following him. I whispered a spell, bringing my guiding winds up. It tugged me this way and that until I was out of town and heading into the forest.

"Tenacious, aren't you?" Percival purred from behind me.

I whirled, then shied back. He held a glowing, icy orb in his hands. Two monster wolves flanked him on either side, their orange eyes focused on me while their tails swished. I glanced around quickly, but it seemed like those two wolves were the only ones there.

"Surprised, Harper?" Percival cooed. "This is far from what you expected, isn't it? Too bad you won't have any answers before you die. It'll be the tragic mystery of Moonhaven, a town slaughtered by wolves who disappeared without a trace."

He laughed and pointed at me. The two wolves sprang forward silently.

I threw my hands out, palms toward them. I shouted an incantation and fire burned from my skin. It arced through the air and melted the first wolf. The second dodged and retreated, growling. Its hair stood on end.

Percival's eyes widened. "Impossible!"

"Guess you're not the only witch in town," I spat at him. I crouched, drawing my flames closer around me. "I understand more about what you've done here than you know. Unfortunately for you, David told me enough."

Percival's face twisted. "You didn't even know him!"

"I didn't need to. I'm a Nightshade. Our specialties are fire and death," I told him, smirking.

The second wolf attacked suddenly. I dodged the attack, whipping my flames around. They whipped against the wolf, and it vanished in sparkles of water vapor that fluttered toward the ground. I straightened and faced Percival again.

"We know the truth now. Your plan won't work. We know you're the one who attacked David. If you send your wolves into town, the only thing that'll happen is that you'll be guilty of more murders."

Percival laughed, an arrogant, raucous sound. "Oh, but if everyone dies, then it doesn't matter who knows, does it?"

He charged me. I sent my flames at him but a burst of ice cracked through the air. Fire and ice met and canceled each other out. Then Percival threw his glowing orb aside and slammed into me. The breath was knocked out of me, my flames dying at once. He wrapped his hands around my throat and squeezed.

I clawed at his hands, but it did no good. I couldn't even summon my flames again.

"I will not lose everything!" he yelled as he tightened his grip. "David Blackwood should have minded his own business! This town belongs to me. I don't care if I have to kill everyone in it! There will be more people. I'll always be able to turn a profit."

I grabbed a handful of snow and threw it into his face. His head jerked back, and I punched forward, jabbing my thumb into his eye.

Percival howled. His grip on me loosened. I shoved at him, making him topple into the snow. I turned, trying to crawl away while fighting to re-inflate my lungs. My throat burned. I couldn't get air in except in noisy gasps.

"Oh, no you don't," Percival shouted. He grabbed my legs and pulled me back.

He was going to kill me. I wheezed, trying to bring my flames forward. He grabbed my wrist and flipped me back onto my back. The fury and hatred in his eyes sent ice through my blood. The frost swirled nearby and a wolf appeared, crouched in the snow.

A sudden crack filled the air. Percival's eyes widened as he toppled over, both of his hands cradling his skull. Abigail stood behind him, her thermos in hand. She reached for me, her eyes wild with fright.

"Come on, let's get you out of—"

The wolf howled and jumped at her, knocking her over. I let out a hoarse shout as I pulled my flames up and shot them at the wolf. It disappeared, but Abigail didn't move, her eyes shut. A trickle of blood ran down her forehead.

Percival laughed as he staggered back to his feet. "Looks like she was knocked out by her own thermos. No matter. I'll deal with you first and then the old woman. Say goodbye, Harper Nightshade."

CHAPTER 6
A WARM WINTER'S NIGHT

I inched backward as my flames fizzled out. Percival's eyes were blazing as he stalked toward me like one of his wolves.

Just as I was dredging up the last of my strength, a flurry of footsteps hailed the approach of another person. We both turned. Liam burst through the trees and smashed into Percival. They went flying, and I cried out through my bruised throat. They rolled through the snow, grappling with each other.

I crawled to Abigail. Her skin was grey and cold, but she was breathing. I grabbed the thermos, surprised at the weight of it, and turned, ready to hurl it toward Percival.

Liam was on top, pinning him to the ground. Percival's face pressed into the snow as he weakly thrashed. I waited, my heart in my throat, for further wolves to appear. They didn't. Liam was currently cuffing Percival's hands behind his back. All around us, the frost melted.

The glowing orb he'd had before lay nearby, cracked down the middle. Abigail must have broken it when she fell… and with it, Percival lost his ability to use the magic inside. It was the only explanation I could come up with.

I checked Abigail's head, finding that she was bleeding pretty badly. I pulled off my jacket and put it over her.

How was I going to explain any of this to anyone?

I'll figure it out later. Sirens pierced the night as Liam dragged Percival to his feet. He tilted his head and nodded in satisfaction.

"I'm going to get this slimeball to the cruiser and come back for you; the ambulance will be here soon."

"Thanks," I murmured shakily. "Hurry, I don't enjoy being out here by myself."

Liam's gaze lingered on mine. He opened his mouth as though to say something... then closed it and shoved Percival through the trees. I tucked my jacket tighter around Abigail, hoping that she'd be okay. She saved my life, again. I didn't know what I'd do if it ended up costing her everything.

"Please be okay," I whispered to her, wishing that healing was among my skills. "Please, Abigail. Please be okay."

* ✳ ❋ ✳ *

Ella squeezed my hands as we sat in the hospital waiting room. She had, apparently, woken suddenly only minutes before we brought Abigail in. From the sounds of it, her waking coincided perfectly with when my showdown with Percival happened.

"I can't wait any longer," she said, standing. "I'm going to—Doctor Rika. Is Abigail okay?"

She raced forward as Moonhaven's only resident doctor, Rika Furukawa, entered the waiting room. We were lucky to have transit doctors come through, but everyone knew Doctor Rika. She smiled at Ella. I hurried to join them. A smile was a good sign, right?

"She's awake and responding well to all our tests. I believe she may have a mild concussion, so I want to keep her under supervision for a while longer. She's asking about both of you."

The hospital bay doors opened. A handful of paramedics came in with Liam following them. They pushed a stretcher. Ella grabbed my arm as we stepped to one side.

"Middle-aged male in a hypothermic state," one paramedic said.

"Get him to room four. Betsy, I'm going to need help," Rika said, growing professional at once.

She hurried after the paramedics while Liam stopped next to Ella and me. I gasped as the man was wheeled past. His skin was ashy and his eyes closed, but I recognized that face.

Ella yanked at my arm in her excitement. "David Blackwood! He's alive?"

"When I took Percival to the station for booking, I found I had an anonymous note on my desk, telling me where to find him. He was tied up in an old wolf's den. He's lucky we've been having warmer nights lately," Liam said, running his hand through his short hair distractedly. "Being as deep as he was in the ground saved his life. A few more hours with the frost tonight…"

I let out a shaky breath and squeezed Ella's hand. "Why don't you go tell Abigail the news? She'll want to know he's okay."

"Abigail's awake?" Liam asked eagerly.

"Yeah."

He looked dead on his feet, so I sent him to sit down and got a coffee for him. He accepted it gratefully and took a long sip.

"There's still a lot that doesn't add up. Who left that note? Why would they do that, rather bring David back themselves?" Liam said. He looked up at me, searching, as though he expected I was the one who left it.

"I don't know anything about that." But I had a suspicion.

That icy ball that Percival had could have been a connector. Something that was using David's life force to enhance Percival's magic. It made sense why the apparitions of David I saw were so strange. He hadn't acted like a spirit, because he wasn't dead.

David himself might have left that note when Percival's power over him broke.

"I'm glad that Abigail is okay," Liam murmured at last. "And Percival is locked up. I think he must have been heading into the forest to finish David off when you interrupted him, which you shouldn't have done. You could have been killed."

His gaze flitted over the bruises on my neck.

"I had to," I told him.

Liam took another sip of coffee. "I guess you did, didn't you? I'm just glad you're okay."

"I'm glad you're okay, too," I said, blushing. We sat in a comfortable silence. I had a feeling that our relationship would not be quite so frosty from here on out.

The End

Did you enjoy *Let it Snow*?

Please consider rating it on <u>Goodreads</u>, <u>Bookbub</u> or your favorite retailer. Reviews help me reach new readers.

Read all the books in the Cozy Mystery Samplers.

Read all the stories

Jane and Kennedy Daniels Mysteries

Pine Grove Mysteries

Wilma Wade Holiday Mysteries

Mike and Maddie Mysteries

Mystic Moonhaven Mysteries

Annie Archer Paranormal Mysteries

Join my Newsletter for updates and giveaways!

www.daisylandishromance.com